Barn Door to HELL
Lucas Mangum

Copyright © 2024 by Lucas Mangum

All rights reserved.

No portion of this book may be reproduced in any form without written permission from the publisher or author, except as permitted by U.S. copyright law.

ISBN: 9798869000422

For Alvin Schwartz and Stephen Gammel.

Acknowledgements

Barn Door to Hell is the sort of book I always wanted to write, a synthesis of themes and tropes I've explored in the past, presented in a more refined way. For inspiration, I turned toward films like *Blood Harvest, Hack-O-Lantern,* and *Invasion of the Blood Farmers*—microbudget works that feel more like dreams of horror fans committed to video than anything cinematic. I also took cues from the books of Bryan Smith and Judith Sonnet.

It was written between April 2023 and Mar 2024.

Prologue

The door to the dark bedroom slid across the carpet with a trembling wheeze. Sixteen-year-old Lydia West turned her face toward the new opening, a crack that was only a shade lighter than the bedroom. A shadow stood near the bottom, clogging the space between the door and its frame. Someone was standing there, watching her. Her mind lingered so close to the edge of sleep, the black shape could've been anyone. Any*thing*.

The exhaustion in her limbs threatened to keep her prone on the bed as the door opened wider. The shadowy figure took one tentative step into the room's engulfing darkness. She could hear the figure's deep, heavy breathing. If such breathing were on the other end of a phone call, she would've thought it was some pervert stroking himself off to the voice of a teenage girl.

That the breather was instead a dark shape standing in her bedroom doorway ignited electric impulses of panic inside the most primitive recesses of her brain. The fatigue in her arms and legs began to flicker away. She made fists under the down comforter and mentally measured the distance from her bed to the window. It was a two-story drop, if she got to it fast enough. She considered holding her breath like some child afraid of the snaggle-toothed vampire hiding in her closet.

The shadowy figure reached forward and pressed a small, spidery hand against the wall. In less than a second, light splashed over the whole of her room, and she yelped. She cut herself off just short of a scream when the light illuminated the figure's familiar features.

"Damn it, Alvin," she said in a harsh whisper. "You scared the shit out of me. What are you doing?"

"Really? You pooped the bed?"

She snatched one of her pillows and hurled it at her little brother. "You know what I mean!"

He plopped down on the edge of her bed. "I can't sleep."

"Well, it's past your bedtime, so keep trying."

"Why are you awake, then?"

"I was about to fall asleep, but then I noticed some creep standing in my room watching me."

Eight-year-old Alvin lifted his shoulders in an innocent shrug. "I was just checking if you were awake."

"I'm awake."

"I know."

The siblings looked at each other. At first, they were expressionless, but then they burst out laughing. When they got the chuckles out of their systems, she leaned forward to muss his hair.

"So, what do you want to do, kiddo?"

He shrugged again. "I dunno."

She flashed him a devilish smile. "I think I have an idea."

His face scrunched up like a broken accordion. "Oh, what?"

Lydia put her feet on the floor and scooted toward her brother. "What if we checked it out?"

"The barn?" he almost shouted.

"Shh. Yes, the barn."

"I don't know."

She put her hand on his knee. "Come on. It makes sense. You're scared, and I'm going to show you there's nothing to be afraid of."

"Really?" He sounded even younger when he said it, like a boy half his age.

"Of course," she said. "What are big sisters for?"

***

Under the sickle-shaped moon, they crept along the side of the house where the goats paced in their pen. The corn stalks surrounding the farm swayed like lanky Christmas carolers who couldn't sing, only hiss and rustle. A nearby animal screeched, and Alvin's grip on Lydia's hand tightened, squeezing her fingers together. She winced and started to pull away.

"You're hurting me!"

"What *was* that?"

"I don't know. Sounded like a possum or something."

"Or something?" His grip tightened again.

"Just. Relax."

He kept a firm hold on her hand for a two count, then loosened his grip. When they reached the pen's fence, the goats came over, expecting a midnight snack.

"What are we doing?" Alvin asked.

"Well, we need to bring a sacrifice." She opened the gate enough for one of the kids to scuttle through before closing it again. "How else are we supposed to know for sure there's nothing in there?"

"But what if there is? What if it eats the goat?"

Lydia looped a length of rope around the little goat's neck. "The goat's gonna be fine." She pulled the rope taut and looked in the direction of the barn. "*We're* going to be fine."

He squared his shoulders and tried to relax his face. She could tell he was trying to look strong for his big sister. His eyes held a softness, though—a doe-eyed vulnerability that told her he wanted to be anywhere but out here, even with her by his side speaking her little reassurances.

The goat let out a bleat and tried chewing on the pocket of her pajama bottoms. She marched toward the barn, rope in one hand, her little brother's hand in the other. The gravel crunched under their feet like rock candy as they approached the barn.

The structure loomed over them. With its red paint rendered gray in the moonlight, it looked less like a manmade object and more like something arcane. From nature but unnatural. An angular symbol was scratched into the wood on the door, crossing over the jamb and onto the neighboring wall. Lydia had once asked Grandpa Al about the symbol, and he'd blamed it on vandals. At night, its presence only added to the barn's otherworldly aura.

She steeled herself with a deep breath and exhaled slowly as if blowing out an excessive number of candles.

"What is it?" Alvin asked.

"Nothing."

"You're scared!" He pulled his hand away from hers. "I want to go back inside."

"I'm not. And no, you can't go back inside. We're already here."

"Lydia ..."

"It's okay. Come on. Hold the goat." She handed him the rope, and he took it in a tentative fist.

She pulled the keyring out of her pocket and found the key marked with a B for barn. The goat bleated as she slid the key into the slot and turned it. Alvin shifted his weight from one foot to the other as Lydia unspooled the thick chain. She pulled open the left door, and it made a sound like a yawning skeleton. A dual odor of hay and animal shit wafted from the opening.

The goat tried circling behind Alvin's legs. Alvin spun and side-stepped so he wouldn't get tangled in the rope. The moonlight illuminated no more than a few feet into the barn, leaving the rest of the inside in deep shadows. Lydia replaced the keyring and produced a flashlight from her opposite pocket. When she flicked it on, the beam spotlighted the straw that covered the barn's floor. She moved the beam back and forth.

"See," she said. "Nothing to be afraid of. Just hay, hay, and more hay."

The goat bleated in reply and tried again to encircle Alvin's legs. Alvin evaded again, this time stepping forward. Realizing he'd set foot in the barn, he stumbled backward and bumped into the goat. The animal bleated and scurried out from under Alvin with such force that the boy fell to his butt and released the rope.

"Ow!"

The goat jetted, dragging the rope with it into the barn. It stood in the middle of hay-covered floor, turned to face Lydia and Alvin, its elongated pupils gleaming in the flashlight beam. Another bleat escaped its lips as Lydia pulled Alvin to his feet.

Around the goat's hoofs, the hay began to ripple.

"Uh, Lydia," Alvin said.

Lydia saw it—she just didn't believe it. It looked like massive fingers rising from the ground on each side of the goat. Eight of them. No, ten. They *were* fingers. Huge fingers. They closed around the goat, interlacing like praying hands.

The goat squirmed, kicking its legs and thrashing its head back and forth. The rope whipped around right along with it. The animal's escalating cries sounded almost human. Like a crying, screaming child.

It dawned on her that those cries were not coming from the goat alone. Alvin had hit the ground a second time and was sliding toward the inside of the barn. A braided tentacle composed solely of hay was snaked around his ankle and pulling him in toward the writhing goat, which was now spitting blood and sunken to its knees.

"Lydia, help me!" Alvin screamed.

Lydia dropped to her hands and knees and scrambled after her little brother's dragging form. Her hands pressed into the hay, and it wormed between her fingers. It felt *alive*.

Two instincts warred inside her. One screamed at her to push up from the ground and scramble away from the living hay. Another beseeched her to save her much smaller brother—her brother who was only out here because of her. She sprang to her feet but simultaneously lunged forward. The move threw her to her belly, knocking the wind from her lungs, but her hand closed around Alvin's wrist.

"Help me, please!" he shrieked.

The goat was dead now. Its legs were bent at unnatural angles with broken-off bones sticking out of bloody holes in the fur. Its eyes were rolled back, its tongue lolling and swollen.

The hay beneath Lydia continued to ripple and writhe. Tendrils of it crawled up her sides like groping hands. She clenched her teeth and snapped her other hand around Alvin's forearm. She worked herself to her knees, playing tug-o'-war with the tentacle gripping Alvin's ankle. By some miracle, she found her feet. A cry shredded its way up her throat and escaped her lips, part exertion, part frustration, all terror.

Something bit into her forearm. The bright flash of pain made her release her hold. It was instinctive, and she cursed herself for it immediately. A second tentacle had slashed a crimson valley into her forearm. Blood streamed from the wound as the first limb dragged Alvin deeper into the barn, shackling him beside the goat, which was now submerged up to its neck and vomiting its blood-slicked guts. A length of bulbous intestine dangled from its jaws like a bloated, elephantine caterpillar. Something dark and mashed leaked from a rip in the side of it, reminding her of overcooked corned beef hash.

The tentacle holding Alvin jerked him upward, taking him six feet into the air. Eight feet. Ten.

He cried out to his sister again. A prolonged desperate plea for her—the closest thing to a mother-figure he knew—to save him from this awful monster that should only exist in his nightmares.

The back of his head smacked the edge of the hay loft, and his eyes went dead. His limbs slackened in the moment before the tentacle brought him back down with a whoosh of air and slammed him to the floor.

Several more of the tendrils broke through the surface around him, surrounding him like a cage of gold and sinew. He lifted his head, semiconscious, as if he were waking from a dream. Spotting Lydia, some life returned to his eyes. He opened his mouth to say something more but could only cough out a pathetic cry.

The tips of the tendrils turned toward him and jutted downward. All ten of them impaled him simultaneously, ripping through flesh and clothing, tunneling through his ribs with a cacophony of crunching bones. The pain widened his eyes and brought forth a final shrill scream from his lips. Blood came with it, drooling down his chin like scarlet broth. His limbs thrashed as if they didn't yet know how hopeless it was to fight, and he sank into the roiling sea of dead plant matter.

Lydia blubbered as she backpedaled. The straw continued to undulate. A red spot spread across the surface where Alvin and the goat had been dragged below. Her feet stuttered to a stop, and she froze as denial set in.

No way. No fucking way had she not only learned that everything she'd heard about her grandparents was true but now her little brother was dead. This could only be a nightmare.

Monsters weren't even real. And yet, they were.

One of them lived right here in the barn.

And now it was reemerging. Pulsating beneath the hay like magma. Causing the surface to bubble and part like a biblical sea. A dark figure emerged from the crevasse, backlit by a nuclear orange glow. The same luminescence flickered in its eyes. The dark figure was small, child sized.

"No," Lydia said, barely above a whisper.

She pointed the flashlight at the figure's face. Her brother had changed in the short time he spent under the hay. He now resembled a scarecrow, with tufts of hay stuffed into every orifice, including the wounds punched into his torso by the tendrils. Every strand billowed with animation as if blowing in the wind. His face had lost all moisture and color, making his head resemble a gray oversized prune.

Pieces of the goat had been fused to him by the remaking hands beneath the hay. Two of the hooves were stuck into his belly, kicking feebly in the air. A third had been rammed up his rectum. From the entry point leaked a chunky syrup of blood and shit. His left fist was stuffed inside the ragged neck beneath the goat's severed head. The decapitated animal's eyes also held the infernal glow. The shredded remains of its bowels clung to its lips and teeth.

He and the goat opened their mouths wider with a duet of screeching cries. The disharmonious notes ignited Lydia's eardrums with agony. Panic and self-preservation made her spin on her heel and explode into a sprint. The hellish cries of her brother and the goat puppet mounted on his fist couldn't fade fast enough behind her. They seemed to follow her, as if each offending set of lips was sailing after her, levitating right beside her ears.

Where before she and Alvin crept around the side of the house, Lydia now ran alone. As she reached the front of the house, she risked a look over her shoulder. The screaming had stopped, but her brother's ruined body was giving chase. It moved with a deliberate certainty, a knowledge that it would catch up to her eventually. That there was nothing she could do to prevent this fate.

Lydia mounted the front stoop and pushed her way through the door. She fell headlong into the house and kicked the door shut behind her.

Finding her feet, she took care to engage the lock before turning and running smackdab into her grandmother's chest. The older woman's arms encircled her.

"It's okay, dear," said Magdalena West. "You're safe now."

"No, it's not okay," Lydia shrieked, pushing away from her grandmother. She saw Grandpa Al standing in the room too. He was holding a hunting rifle in a white-knuckle, shaky grasp. "Alvin is dead and now he's ... he's ..."

"Your grandmother's right," Grandpa Al said. "You go on upstairs."

Chapter 1

Carson Reid looked up from her phone, and the weathered sign welcoming her family to Reaper's Bend drew her gaze. The old woodcut image depicted a farmer standing in a field of wheat and wielding a scythe. Even with the fading paint and splitting wood, Carson could make out an expression on the man's rugged face that seemed too cheerful for someone toiling in the fields.

"I can't believe that's really the name of the town," Carson said.

She met the gaze of the wood-carved man. His irises were faded entirely, leaving only the black pupils.

"It makes sense if you think about it," her father said.

The station wagon drove past the sign, and Carson watched it grow smaller in the distance over the mountain of luggage and boxes in the back. The man's grin lingered in her mind's eye as her father slowed the vehicle and the engine groaned in protest. Change rattled in the cupholders as the stretch of pavement lost its smoothness. The sign and the road were the only manmade structures in the immediate vicinity. On either side of the moving vehicle, densely packed trees stretched for miles in all directions. Even with the windows up, Carson could smell fallen pine needles and dead, wet leaves.

"It's creepy," Carson said.

"Says the girl who wanted to interview the director of those *Insidious* movies for her school paper," her mother said. "I swear our daughter is just a bundle of contradictions."

She glared at her mom, who was watching her in the rearview, daring her to say something. "Just because I like horror movies doesn't mean I want to live in one. Besides, he liked my tweet, so I didn't think it hurt to ask. I was, like, fifteen."

"It never hurts to ask," her father said. "And it never hurts to try something new."

"Like coming to a small town with a creepy name because my parents want to take up farming? Gee, Dad. Nice pivot."

"Just dadding at my daddiest," he said and turned briefly to flash her a grin.

She huffed but couldn't suppress a grin of her own.

"I think it's going to be nice," her mother said for what must have been the millionth time since her parents had made their decision. Almost like she was trying to convince herself.

"Yeah, totally," Carson said and went back to her phone. She found a Ghostmane mix on Spotify and turned up the volume.

She rested her head against the cool window as the car rounded a curve. There were more trees. Sometimes, a collapsing wooden shed or the stone shell of an old building broke up the monotony on the outskirts of her family's new stomping grounds.

They entered town, cruising below a banner affixed to two electrical poles. The banner had *Barnyard Days Festival* and some dates printed on it.

Main Street looked like something you'd see on a postcard from a bygone era. Every business was either independently owned or governmental. There wasn't a franchise name in sight. They passed a diner, a grocery store named Holland's, a tavern called Clippers, a post office, the library, and a taxidermist. The small-town sights cut a stark contrast to the trap metal that blared on her headphones.

After Main Street, it was back to trees, farmland, and winding, hilly thoroughfares. Almost as if the town were an accident. An anomalous growth that nature would soon correct. Eventually, the car slowed and turned onto a gravel driveway that took them down toward a farmhouse made of stone and wood paneling.

The driveway looped around a dried-up mud pit, and Carson found herself wishing like a child that her father would drive around the loop and head back toward the road, this whole trip to the middle of nowhere just some elaborate joke. He stopped the station wagon in front of the house and cut the engine.

Carson paused the music and took off her headphones. By the time she put her phone in her bag and dragged herself out of the back seat, her father already had the hatch open and was unloading the largest suitcase. They'd owned it for as long as she could remember, and it always reminded her of something you'd use to hide a collection of severed limbs.

Carson grabbed one of the boxes and headed for the door. Her mother was standing beside the car with her arms crossed, staring at the mud hole at the center of the yard.

"I guess that was our pond," her mother said.

"That's all right," her father said. "Maybe that can be one of your projects."

Carson put down the box by the door and waited for her father to come with the keys. "That's true, Mom. You do like aqua scaping."

Lacey Reid cast a scowl her daughter's way. Carson turned away before her mother could retort with more than a look. They both knew there was a world of difference between designing an aquarium and maintaining a pond.

Her father reached the front stoop and let go of the suitcase before fishing in his pockets for the keys. "Don't give her a hard time. She and I may be on the same page about moving here, but she left behind a lot more than I did."

"What about what I left behind?" Carson said.

Her father attempted a smile when he reached past her and stuck the key in the lock. The deadbolt disengaged with a heavy tumble, and he opened the door to reveal a dusty, dark hallway. Several of the fixtures had been pulled down, and the beams were exposed along one side of the wall. A smashed mirror lay in the center of the floor—a bad omen if Carson ever saw one. Calling this place a "fixer-upper" would be too kind. Carson cast a look at her mother, who had grabbed a smaller suitcase from the trunk and was wheeling it toward the house.

"Here we are," Dale Reid said. "Home, sweet home."

"You're such a dad," Carson said.

Dale grabbed the heavy suitcase and heaved it over the threshold. "I'll take that as a compliment."

Carson rolled her eyes and picked up the box. Her mother came to her side and took a deep breath.

"You okay, Mom?"

"I'm just glad we finally made it, that's all."

"The power's out," Dale called from somewhere in the house. "I'm going to try the breakers."

"Great," Carson and her mother said in unison.

Chapter 2

"Hey," Carson said into her phone. She was sitting on the edge of the tub in the upstairs bathroom. She had the camera pointed down at her from a high angle and her thumb pressed down on the record button. In her other hand, she held a burning candle in an antique saucer she found in one of the cabinets. The flames reflected red against her cheeks and the cracked tile behind her. "In case you're wondering about the candle, our brand-new house ... has no power. It's less than ideal, but at least it looks cool on camera." She let out a heavy sigh that she only slightly exaggerated for the video. "I miss everyone already."

"Carson?" her father called.

"Time's up," she said to the camera.

She stopped recording, wrote a short caption dramatizing the grimness of her situation and started to assign the relevant tags. #movingin #fixerupper #missingmyfriends #worstdayever

"Carson, did you hear Dad?"

She stopped typing. "Be right there."

She got up from the tub and uploaded the video to TikTok on her way out of the bathroom. She slipped the phone in her pocket so she could guard the candle's flame. Its heat felt pleasant against her palm as she came downstairs and stood in the hallway.

"Hey, Mom. Dad. What's up?"

"What do you want on your pizza?" her father asked from the spacious living room, pulling open a massive shade. The window he stood at was tall and let in enough illumination that Carson didn't need the candle. "We're ordering from a place called Charley-O's."

Her phone buzzed in her pocket. She blew out the candle and set it down on the ledge separating the living room from the kitchen. "I don't think that name's Italian."

Mom looked up from scrubbing one of the counters and put her hands on her hips. Her dark brown hair hung in her face, and her cheeks were pink. "Do you always have to be a critic?"

"I'm just pointing out the obvious. I'll take pepperoni and anchovies."

"So, you want an individual-sized?" Dad asked.

She took out her phone and deadpanned, "What, you guys don't want to share?"

"It sounds like *you* don't want to share, smarty pants," Mom said, but she was smiling.

"You know it." She opened the TikTok notification. It was a private message from someone named Jennie Silva. The profile picture showed a smooth bronze face framed by sensuous waves of brown hair with golden highlights.

HEY. I SEE YOU'RE IN REAPER'S BEND AND NEW IN TOWN. SORRY ABOUT YOUR POWER OUTAGE, THAT SUCKS! ANYWAY, I CHECKED OUT YOUR PROFILE AND WAS WONDERING IF YOU'D BE INTERESTED IN COMING OUT TO HELP ON AN INDEPENDENT HORROR FILM SHOOT TONIGHT. I'M THE DIRECTOR AND I'VE DONE SOME WORK YOU MIGHT HAVE SEEN. HERE'S MY IMDB PAGE. IF INTERESTED, LET ME KNOW AND I'LL DM YOU THE ADDRESS. NO WORRIES IF NOT. I JUST FIGURED IT DIDN'T HURT TO ASK. PEACE, JENNIE.

Carson felt her face involuntarily brighten, and she began to type out an enthusiastic response.

"*Some*one's in a better mood," Mom said.

"*Some*one's already making new friends," Carson said and finished typing her message. She hit send and looked up at Dad. "Can I borrow the car after pizza?"

"That depends on who your new friends are," he said.

"Dad, seriously?"

"Not serious at all." He winked at her. "You can borrow the car if you help us with the rest of these windows. I'm glad you're already meeting people. You'll have a new network in no time."

"That doesn't mean I've changed my mind about moving here."

"Oh, of course not," Mom said.

After they finished opening all the blinds and curtains, the house had enough natural light to get around without fumbling. It was cold, though, and night would have its own challenges. It would be good to get out of the house.

The pizza came, and they ate as a family. When they finished, there was still time before she had to head out, so Carson decided to explore outside.

She crested the rolling hill behind her new home. Dead grass crinkled under her feet, and a cool breeze blew against her face. The air smelled different out this way. Earthy but not lush, it reminded her of flowers sitting too long in a vase—most of the water dried up, the leaves and petals wilted, with gnats weaving between the mottled stems. She supposed some people might find that pleasant, but not her—she felt much more at home with the concrete and car exhaust of Stamford.

She stopped walking at the center of the hilltop where her dad said their property ended, and she surveyed her surroundings. She had to admit she liked the quiet. She less appreciated how dead everything looked on her family's new land. If this were anything other than a whole new house, she would've given her parents three months before they threw in the towel. They would be here for the long haul, though, and it was going to be a lot of work. Except ...

The land on the other side of the hill looked like it existed in a completely different climate than her family's new farm. The grass was a vibrant emerald green and grew past her ankles. All the trees bore thick manes of leaves, even this close to autumn. Carson couldn't tell why the foliage was so rich on that side and so sparse on her family's side.

She spotted a cornfield, rows upon rows of the stuff, stretching up another hill before stopping at another wall of trees. These trees were less lush than the ones closer to this side of the hill.

At the center of the fertile land stood an old farmhouse even more rundown than her new abode. Shutters hung off their hinges beside dirty, cracked windows. Leaf-choked gutters sagged at the edges of a weather-beaten roof. The house looked like something neglected for half a century or more, despite the obvious abundance of the cornfield. There was a stone well out front, and behind the home loomed a red barn.

The barn's paint was peeling and faded, but its bones looked strong. The structure didn't sway or sag, and the wood showed no signs of rot. It could've been a trick of the distance. Up close, the boards could have been termite-eaten and splintered, but Carson didn't think they would be.

The barn cast a long shadow, stretching toward the cornfield like a dark gray hand. The shadow made her stomach tighten with anxiety for reasons she couldn't at first place. When she looked up at the sun, the source of her unease dawned on her. It was late afternoon, and the sun hung in the western section of the sky. The barn cast its shadow toward it

Chapter 3

Sheriff Regis Jones pulled his cruiser into a parking spot in front of the Tucker County Sheriff's station in Reaper's Bend. The building was a brown-brick polygon lit with light tubes that buzzed and flickered. Metal letters above the front door denoted its designation. Located adjacent to Main Street, it was accessible via a side street between the post office and the taxidermist.

The sharp chill in the mid-September air hit Regis like a stiff slap to the face as soon as he opened the cruiser door. He hastily removed his hat and stepped briskly into the office. The cool air lingered until he shut the door. The air in the office was stuffy, but the warmth from the vents more than compensated for it.

Daisy Keener sat behind the desk, and her deeply lined face brightened when she saw Regis come in. The expression made her look like a woman half her age. "Hey, Batman. How are the streets of Gotham?"

"Cold and quiet."

"They won't be quiet for long."

"You don't need to remind me. Is everyone here?"

"Everyone but Phillip and the new guy."

"Of course," Regis said through gritted teeth. "Did he give you an ETA?"

"Just that they were on their way."

"Did he say what the holdup is?"

"He didn't provide that information, even though I told him it would be helpful and appreciated."

Regis sighed. "How do I get him to respect me, Daisy?"

"You can always take him out back and smack him around some," she said with a gentle shrug. "He's as old as me, so I bet it's been a while since he got a good honest-to-God beating."

"I can't imagine you ever needed the sense knocked into you."

"That's because you didn't know me when I was young."

Regis chuckled despite his annoyance with Phillip's tardiness and the example it was setting for Avery Joel. If Phillip's trainee thought it was okay to walk all over him, what hope did Regis have for filling his father's shoes? Despite these concerns, Daisy always had a knack for cheering him up a little. It had been that way since he was a boy and she used to give him lollipops on the sly whenever Dad brought him to the station.

"There's that smile," she said. "Now, go back there and hold court. Phillip and the rookie will be here soon enough. If you really want to make an example out of him, you can always have a pop quiz at the end."

"Was that how Dad handled him?"

"I already told you how your dad would've handled him."

Regis wasn't sure beating up on the elderly was something he wanted as part of his legacy as Sheriff. He knocked on Daisy's desk. "Send him back when he gets here."

"You bet," she said.

Regis entered the conference room at the station, and the chatter between the attending deputies ceased. He sat down at the head of the table and leaned forward to scan the faces of everyone seated. Eighteen deputies in all, a mix of young and middle-aged faces. Some men and women he knew personally, others mere acquaintances.

"Everyone okay tonight?" he asked. There were several murmured responses. "All right, great. Now, everyone knows this weekend is the Barnyard Days Festival, so we're going to need all hands on deck."

The door unlatched and opened behind him. Avery Joel, the new deputy, scooted in. Pink clouded his cheeks when he met Regis's gaze. Regis couldn't be mad at the kid, though. He was still in training. When Deputy Phillip Lee entered the room, Regis fixed him with an admonishing stare. Rather than dress him down in front of everyone, he decided to stay on task and address the insubordination afterward.

"As I was saying, this is an all-hands situation. Since this is the only time of year my office asks this of you, I know that won't be a problem."

Phillip whispered something in his trainee's ear. Whatever it was prompted Avery to look down and to the side. Regis thought he heard *Sheriff Blazing Saddles* among the words spoken. That was a nickname Phillip had given to Regis's father, the first Black sheriff to serve in the very White Tucker County. If he heard it, some of the others in the room also undoubtedly did. He couldn't let it fly.

"Something you want to share with the rest of the class, Deputy?" Regis asked.

"Of course not, Sheriff. Just letting Deputy Avery here know this is your favorite time of year."

Regis felt his chest go cold, all notions of confronting Phillip's racism forgotten to make room for unpleasant memories. Memories he wasn't entirely sure weren't merely nightmares.

"Funny," he said in a tone he did his best to keep neutral.

"Why do you hate the festival so much?" Deputy Judith Cane asked. "I think it's fun."

"Maybe I'll tell you next year," Regis said.

"You said that last year," Judith said.

"Yeah, maybe I did. And maybe I'll say the same thing every year. It's not important. What is important is that over the next few days, there will be a lot more activity in Reaper's Bend than there usually is. It's our job to make sure the whole place doesn't fall apart. Does anyone have any questions about where they need to be or when they need to be there?"

When no one raised their hand or spoke up, he dismissed the meeting. Everyone got up to leave, but he stopped Phillip and Avery at the door. "Are you gonna tell me why you were late?"

"Lost track of time; you know how it can be out on the beat," Phillip said with a saccharine grin.

"Uh huh, especially when Nana keeps the coffee refills coming." Regis turned to the rookie. "Isn't that right, Avery?"

The new deputy blushed an even deeper shade than before.

"Thought so. And Phillip?"

The older deputy's smugness didn't falter.

"If I hear you call me or my father 'Blazing Saddles' again, I'm gonna take you out back and smack you around. Clear?"

Phillip looked away but muttered his assent.

Chapter 4

Carson parked the station wagon in front of the colonial located at the edge of the Reaper's Bend suburbs. The house had fat wooden pillars stretching from the roof to the concrete floor of the veranda and caging a stone wall, two windows, and a thick oaken door. Its lawn was well-kept and cleaved down the middle by a concrete path. On one side, a tall tree provided a canopy of tangled branches and leaves like green and yellow flags. A wood-paneled camper van, a sleek blue Subaru, and a blood-red Audi were parked along the street. The porch light glowed like a miniature moon.

She got out and stretched before walking up and knocking on the front door. She heard some yelling from the inside. She couldn't make out the words, but the tones made her neck and shoulders go tense. Aggressive footsteps marched toward the front door before someone yanked it open. The woman on the other side's eyebrows were screwed into an exasperated expression. This wasn't the same person who messaged her but a blonde with a pale complexion and long, hot pink fingernails.

Carson found her voice. "Uh, hi, I'm Carson."

"You were supposed to text," the woman at the door said.

"I'm sorry. I guess I got excited."

"It's fine. We'll just have to do a retake."

The woman turned and walked back into the house. She left the door open, so Carson followed.

The house was mostly gutted on the inside. Devoid of furniture. Most of the floorboards ripped up. She could see that a room down the hallway was brightly illuminated. She and the woman who let her in entered the lighted room.

"Jennie," the greeter said. "The girl you messaged is here."

The twenty-something woman standing over a camera monitor turned toward Carson and fixed onto her with a dark, narrow gaze. Her skin was so smooth it looked air-brushed—a TikTok filter made flesh. "I thought you worked on shoots before," she said.

Carson's stomach knotted instantly. "I ..."

"Never mind. Just remember to text next time. I had literally just called 'action' when you knocked. Screwed everything up, but whatever. I'm Jennie." She pointed at the woman who let Carson in. "That's Ashley."

A man standing beside one of the lighting rigs held up his hand in a wave. He had long gray hair, thick-rimmed glasses, and a paunch that stretched his black Mötley Crüe T-shirt. He introduced himself as Kenny.

"Most of the equipment is his," Jennie said, and Carson got the impression she was making an excuse for his being there.

"Hi," Carson said and tried to smile.

On the lone piece of furniture, a young man with black hair and a five o'clock shadow sat with his tan, muscular arms around a woman with auburn hair and dark eye makeup. The man's eyes gave Carson a once over without his partner taking notice.

"I'm Gabriel," he said. He had a sultry, sexy voice, but she had anything but romance on her mind.

"Ava," the lady beside him said in a flat tone.

"Okay!" Jennie clapped her hands. "Now that the niceties are out of the way, let's get back to work."

"Actually, could we step outside?" Kenny asked. He held up a vape pen and waved it.

Jennie sent him a withering gaze before softening and saying, "Okay, fine. Make it quick."

"Appreciate you, Ms. Awesome Director."

Jennie rolled her eyes as Kenny walked past her into the hallway.

When the door shut, Ava sat up and groaned. "Well, he only looked at my tits *three* times tonight."

"Shit, he looks at my junk all the time," Gabriel said. "It's harmless."

"Ugh, maybe for you." Ava fiddled with her thumbnail. "You'd just kneecap him if he gets too close."

What the hell did I walk into? Carson wondered. She decided to take the subject away from a leering crewmember. "So, what's the movie about?"

Jennie's face considerably brightened. "It's about a killer stalking a neighborhood on Fourth of July as revenge for getting disfigured in a fireworks mishap."

"It's Gabriel and Ava's turn to get slaughtered," Ashley said.

"Right after they get it on, of course," Gabriel said and planted a gentle kiss on Ava's lips.

"But it's, like, feminist because the killer's a woman," Ashley said.

Jennie gave Ashley a one-armed hug and a condescending pat on the shoulder. "Oh, Ashley, you're only reason anyone takes me seriously."

"Come on, you're a genius."

"That sounds cool," Carson said, though she already wanted to leave. "Um, does anyone know anything about the barn behind my house?" she asked.

Jennie's eyebrows furrowed. "What barn?"

"Is it the one off 473?" Ava asked.

"Yeah, it's kind of ... weird."

Gabriel blew out a long breath. "You want my advice, you should move."

Carson choked down a laugh. "What? Why?"

"That's the West place," Jennie said. "There are all sorts of stories about it. It's the whole reason we have that stupid Barnyard Days Festival."

Carson remembered the banner that hung over Main Street. "What kind of stories?"

"It's a bad place," Gabriel said. "Shit's haunted."

"By who?" Carson asked.

"More like, by what." Jennie rolled her eyes. "I mean, it's all bullshit, of course."

"Total bullshit," Ashley echoed.

Carson feigned nonchalance. "Well, what do people say?"

Kenny reentered the space, reeking of weed and nicotine. "You guys talking about the West place?"

Carson made eye contact and pursed her lips, trying to play to the older guy's pervy tendencies. "Do you know anything about it?"

Kenny licked his lips, squared his shoulders, and sucked in his gut. "Yeah, I might know a thing or two." He winked, and she forced a smile. "Long story short, Al West supposedly made a deal with the devil to keep his crops growing when he was about to lose his farm. In exchange, he had to keep *something* in the barn. Something from …" He pointed downwards, indicating hell.

"Are you kidding me?" Carson asked.

"Hey, you asked," Kenny said.

"No, I know. Just …" Carson faced Jennie. "I think this is your movie."

"Excuse you?" Ashley said, her voice sharp and incredulous.

"Why convolute some half-baked slasher movie when you have a very real story right here?"

"My movie isn't half-baked." Jennie's eyes were full of hurt, then her face hardened. "Where do you get off, anyway? Is this how you plan on making friends in your new town?"

"I'm not trying to be a bitch or anything. I'm just surprised. You seem smart and creative. I would think that something like a barn that casts its shadow toward the sun and has *that* story behind it … I can't believe that wouldn't be your go-to idea for an independent horror movie."

Gabriel, Ava, and Kenny were all watching, rapt.

"How do you know she hasn't made that movie yet?" Ashley asked.

Carson didn't take her eyes off Jennie. "Did you?"

Jennie's eyes darted around the room. A muscle worked in her jaw. Her cheeks flushed crimson. "You know what? First, you screw up a take, then you tell me my idea sucks?" She pointed to the door. "Why don't you get the fuck out of here?"

Carson gave sincere thought to apologizing. After all, who did she think she was walking onto a film set and telling people what they should be working on? She was a journalist, not a filmmaker, even though she sometimes made videos. She had meant no offense, but her excitement sometimes made her words run away from her.

Then again, coming here—to this shoot, to this town—was snakebit from the start.

"Yeah, fine. You're right. Maybe I'll just do my own story about the barn. Good luck with *Freedom the Thirteenth* or whatever this piece of shit is called."

Carson spun on her heel and stomped to the door, feeling every eye in the room burning a hole in her back. She stepped outside and let the door fall shut. When she got into the station wagon, she tried to get control of her breath. Tried to notice things to take her mind off how epically bad her first interaction with new people had gone. How it was mostly her fault.

She flexed her hands on the worn leather of the steering wheel. Pressed her back against the seat. Scanned the streets and noted how much darker they'd gotten in such a short amount of time. Watched flying insects madly orbit the streetlights like glitching satellites.

She reached for the knob to turn on the radio. A knock on her window made her jolt and grab the gearshift, ready to put the pedal to the metal if it was some weirdo outside her car with evil intentions. She risked a look out the window. The first thing she noticed was the knocker's hand and its hot pink fingernails. She recognized the fingernails as belonging to the young woman who let her in—Ashley.

She put down the window. "What is it?"

She half-hoped it would be an invite back to the shoot. An olive branch. It wasn't like they had been the most welcoming bunch. From the moment she arrived, it seemed like both Ashley and Jennie wanted her gone. Ashley's face was hard to read in the shadows.

"Do you really want to check out the barn?" Ashley asked.

"Yeah."

"Tonight?"

Carson shrugged one shoulder.

"Can I come?"

Carson took a few seconds to process Ashley's words. "What about Jennie?"

"I'm tired of being her damn attack dog. It was honestly kind of cool to see someone stand up to her."

Carson further considered the other woman's change in demeanor. "Can you take photos and video while I take notes?"

"Yeah, Jennie has me shoot B-roll all the time."

Carson nodded and unlocked the passenger door. "All right. Come on."

Ashley rounded the front of the car and climbed inside. Carson pulled away already feeling better about tonight.

Chapter 5

Clippers was the sort of place that came to mind when someone said the words "dive bar." Bad lighting. Bad music. Bad attitudes. Entering was like walking into the nicotine equivalent of an opium den. Everything stank, and it was hard to see much more than drab silhouettes and flickering neon ads for shitty beer. "The Vengeful One" by Disturbed battered the PA speakers from the jukebox.

Regis found his father slumped in the usual spot at the end of the bar, right near the bathroom. A half-drained pint glass sat in front of him on top of a soaked napkin.

"All right, Dad. Checkout time."

"What?" Abram Jones slurred. "I just got here."

Regis made eyes at Gary the barkeep. "How many has he had?"

"I'm not flagging the sheriff," Gary said.

Abram took a generous gulp, bringing the contents of his glass down to its last few sips.

"Especially not if he's paying his tab, right?" Regis said. Gary held up his hands in a defensive gesture. Regis turned his back on him and put a hand on his father's shoulder. "Come on, Dad. It's time to go."

"Get your hands off me. I don't need nobody's help staying vertical." Regis took his hand away. Abram teetered but stayed on his stool. He gestured to the dregs of his pint. "Gonna let me get my money's worth before you haul me outta here, Sheriff?"

"I should say no."

"But you won't."

Abram tried a grin, but it made him look like a constipated man clenching his teeth while attempting to dislodge an especially stubborn turd. Nothing of the man Regis grew up with lived in that expression. Only a shameful parody. One day, Regis would find out why he did this to himself on such a regular basis. What had changed to make him so utterly give up on himself? He had broached the subject before, more than once, and it had gone less than well.

Abram downed the rest of the glass in one swill. Most of it wound up on his chin and down the front of his shirt. "Oops. Oh well. Closing time?"

"It is for you, Dad. Come on."

Abram slinked off his stool and began to shuffle toward the door. Regis gave Gary a curt nod and followed close behind. The stench of Clippers clung to them like fungus to a moist log.

By the time Regis reached his father's house, Abram was conked out in the passenger seat. Regis left the engine running to keep the car warm. When helping Abram out, the old man babbled something too slurred to understand. Regis kept his arm under Abram's shoulders all the way to the front door.

Inside, Regis didn't turn on any lights, but he did use the flashlight on his phone to navigate the floor safely. As predicted, the place needed a deep clean. Though his father used to be the tidiest man Regis had ever known, that wasn't the case since his retirement.

A lot had changed since his retirement.

They traipsed around discarded articles of clothing, empty beer cans, and God knew what else. Regis hadn't the foggiest idea what his father did during the day before heading to Clippers for the night. It was a sad situation, but who was he to tell a sixty-something-year-old man how to live his life.

He got his father to the bed and helped him out of his coat and shoes. Abram stirred awake and coughed. He spat a wad of something onto the wall above the bedside trashcan. Regis tried not to cringe as the loogie slid down the drywall.

"*Chi-Town Rumble*," Abram slurred.

Regis didn't need to ask his father to clarify. He rooted around for the remote and found it under a fast-food wrapper. His hand and the remote came away greasy.

"Jesus, Dad." He crumbled the wrapper and tossed it in the overfilled bedside bin.

"What?"

Regis could feel a tirade burning at the tip of tongue, but he swallowed every word. "Just get some rest. I'll come by in a few days to help you straighten the place up. Then maybe—"

"You gonna put on my rassling?"

Regis squeezed the remote so hard, it nearly snapped in his hand. Instead, he relaxed his grip and switched on the television.

After he pushed play on the proper program, he covered his father with a comforter. Abram was already snoring, but Regis kept the show playing in case he woke up again. Something about the old wrestling matches kept Abram's mind quiet enough to find rest, giving him the peace reality had so denied him.

Chapter 6

"This where you live?" Ashley asked as Carson pulled into the long gravel driveway off Route 473.

"As of this afternoon. I'm still getting used to it."

The house was still dark, which meant her parents hadn't managed to get the power turned back on yet. It was going to be a cold night, and she longed for her house in the city with its warm bed and access to Netflix.

"Why'd you move?"

Carson drove up to the front of the house. The dried-up pond was a black pit a few short paces from the driver's side door. "My dad wanted to take up farming."

"Do *you* want to take up farming?"

Carson made a sound like she was hacking up a hairball. "God, no. I'm a journalist."

"You're an adult. Why'd you have to move with them?"

"They're helping me while I try to get my career off the ground. Or they were—until they moved me away from my contacts."

Ashley slapped the center console. "Hey, that's okay. We're about to make history by documenting my town's creepy barn. Right?"

Carson contemplated this for a beat, then smiled at her new friend and cut the engine. "Right."

Outside, Carson took her phone from her pocket and opened the notes app. Ashley reached into her bag and took out a sleek camera.

"That looks expensive," Carson said.

"It was. Jennie talked me into buying it."

Carson tried not to roll her eyes. She pointed past her house at a patchy, dry stretch of grass. "It's that way."

They walked along the side of the house. The moon and stars provided ample light. So many stars were visible, like there were more stars than black space.

"I bet the sky didn't look like this in the city," Ashley said.

"No, definitely not."

The visibility of so many celestial bodies caused a wave of something feral to course through Carson. This was wild land, and she was far from home.

She and Ashley began to ascend the hill. When they reached the top, they stopped to catch their breath and take stock. On the other side of the hill, the barn waited. Its red boards and white trim were only shades of gray in the night. She couldn't tell which direction it cast its shadow because all around it was shadow. This new nebulous quality called into question whether she had truly seen the barn casting its shadow toward the sun earlier.

"Hey, Ashley?"

"Yeah?"

"Do people in town say anything about the barn's shadow?"

"Oh yeah. They say it casts a shadow in the wrong direction. I've never seen it. Well, I've seen a photo, but it could've been fake."

"No, it was real. That's what I saw this afternoon."

"Creepy." Neither of them spoke for a five-count. "Maybe this isn't such a hot idea."

Carson couldn't disagree—it was creepy. Even at night, when the phenomenon wasn't as visible, it turned her guts to a bundle of cables. The farmhouse beside the barn looked even more rundown now, a decaying structure set to collapse into the earth at any second. The well out front looked like an eyepiece made of stone. But still, there was the promise of a story, the promise of not letting this uprooting of her life derail her from her course.

"It will be fine," she said. "Come on. We'll get some nice shots, I'll write the piece, and Jennie Silva can eat her heart out." Ashley flashed her a small smile. "Yeah?"

"Let's do it."

"That's the spirit."

The young women walked down the hill, Ashley hugging the camera to her chest like a priceless family heirloom. Carson's thumbs were already working, typing descriptions into her phone that properly captured the ambience of the place at night. When she reached the bottom of the hill, it hit her.

She lowered her phone and looked around. "Oh, God."

"What *is* that?" Ashley asked.

"It smells like actual shit." Carson lifted each foot to check the bottoms of her shoes.

"That's gotta be what it is." Ashley clasped one hand over her mouth and nose. "So gross."

Carson scanned their surroundings for the source of the stench. Her gaze came to rest on the well. "I think it's coming from there."

"From the drinking water?"

Carson drew nearer to the well. She pocketed her phone and covered her mouth and nose with her shirt. Even through the fabric, she smelled it: copious amounts of pungent excrement. Her gag reflex threatened to stage a violent revolt, but she suppressed her gorge with morbid curiosity. She peered over the stone lip of the well and into the blackness below.

"Is it coming from there?" Ashley called from across the yard.

"I can't see anything." A nonanswer, but she wanted to see the source, regardless of how vile it might be. She took her phone back out and shined the flashlight into the inky depths. A thick sludge the color of

Texas crude glistened at the well's bottom. "There's something down there, but it isn't water."

This was good stuff. Already, she could see the piece taking shape. The way she would set the scene. Where she would layer in the background. Some personal asides about this nighttime excursion with her local contact.

Something hissed from the direction of the farmhouse. She pulled her face from the edge of the well, and her shirt collar fell from her face. The stink from the well wafted against her exposed skin, making her gag and take several steps backward.

"Carson?" Ashley said.

She looked at Ashley, then at the house. A shadow filled its door.

Carson switched to reporter mode. "Hi. We didn't mean to disturb you. We didn't think anyone still lived here."

The shadow stepped onto the sagging porch. The weathered boards creaked beneath its steps. The moon and stars partially illuminated the figure, revealing a spider-thin woman with hunched shoulders and a face like an old shoe.

"It's nothing to fret about, dear," the woman said. Though the words were kind, something about their tone and cadence made Carson's skin prickle. "You just moved into that house over the hill. You didn't know any better."

"Yes, ma'am. I was just taking a look around."

Two cats circled the woman's legs. One of them meowed as she glared Ashley's way. "You, though. You ought to know better. Everyone in Reaper's Bend knows this land is cursed."

Carson thought she saw the woman smile. "Is it true, then? What people say?"

The smile broadened, and in the grayness, there was something uncanny about it. "Of course not. Would I be living here if it was?"

The woman shoved the cats back inside with her foot. One of them backed away and hissed. Ashley chuckled nervously. Carson blew out a breath she didn't know she was holding. The stink from the well reminded her that despite the woman's attempt at humor, something was wrong here.

"Is your husband awake?" Carson couldn't quite bring herself to ask about the shadow of the barn.

"My husband's dead. Been gone for quite some time now."

"I'm sorry."

"No need for that. You young ladies want to check out the barn, I reckon."

"No, we can just—" Ashley began.

"It's no trouble."

"Are you sure?" Carson asked, heart fluttering with excitement. "Could I interview you after we have a look around?"

"Not tonight. Even an old bird like me needs her beauty rest."

"Of course, ma'am."

"You don't need to call me ma'am. I'm Magdalena. Maggie or Ms. West will do just fine." She turned to go back inside.

"Will we need a key?" Carson asked. "For the barn, I mean?"

Magdalena cast a final glance over her shoulder. Carson couldn't read it in the deepening gloom. She waited for the woman to say something else, but Magdalena shuffled back inside and closed the door.

"Well, that was ten kinds of weird," Ashley said.

Not untrue, but all Carson heard was *permission*.

"Do you want to wait in the car?"

Ashley shifted her gaze and chewed her lip. "No. We've got to go through with it. Eat your heart out, Jennie Silva, right?"

"Exactly."

Ashley held her camera out like a shield. As they headed toward the barn, she began to film their surroundings. The closer that they got,

Carson buzzed with anticipation. Ashely moved slowly, keeping her hands steady. When they reached the door, Carson noticed a series of eldritch symbols around its frame.

"Are you getting those?" she asked.

"Yeah. Do you know what they mean?"

"I don't know. Maybe some local kids carved them."

"I don't know."

Carson didn't know either, but she wasn't about to say it. They were so close to seeing the inside. She took hold of the polished brass handle, felt its coolness kiss the inside of her palm like the lips of a dead lover. She gave the door a pull.

"It's stuck," she said.

Ashley licked her lips. Kept the camera pointed at the door.

Carson pocketed her phone and took the handle in both hands. She bent her knees and pulled with more oomph than before. With an abrasive scraping sound, the door came free of its frame and yawned open to reveal the barn's insides.

Ashley lowered her camera. "I don't know what I was expecting, but a bunch of hay and some stray tools wasn't it."

"What else do you find in a barn? A gray alien wiping down his flying saucer with a T-shirt rag and a jar of Turtle Wax?"

Ashley laughed. "Well, I wasn't expecting something that ridiculous."

She stepped forward, lifting her camera to get footage of the inside. One foot landed on the hay-covered floor. The dried vegetation whispered under the pressure. She stepped all the way inside, aimed her camera up at the ladder leading to the hay loft. She went further in, and Carson watched, proud of her new friend for shaking off whatever heebie-jeebies the barn might have inspired.

Then Ashley gasped and backpedaled. She dropped her camera during the escape and didn't stop to catch her breath until she reached Carson's side. Until she was back outside the barn.

"What is it?" Carson asked.

"Something rubbed against my ankle. I think it was a snake."

Carson ran the light beam from her phone over the lumpy straw floor. She detected no movement. She and Ashley exchanged glances.

"Oh, damn it," Ashley said. "I left my camera in there."

"I'll get it, if you need me to. Any snake in there will be more afraid of us than we are of it."

"I don't know. Snakes freak me out pretty bad. Ugh, Jennie may be a bitch, but she never led me into a snake's nest."

Carson took a breath to keep cool. "I'll get it. Don't worry. It's sort of my fault you're out here anyway."

Ashley gave Carson an apologetic smile. "I'm sorry."

"No, I'm sorry. Wait out here."

Carson tromped into the barn. She made her footsteps as heavy as possible so any snakes in the straw would know she was coming and get out of her way. When she came within three paces of the camera, the hay rose up around it, closed over it, pulled it under.

"What. The. Fuck."

Between the strands at her feet, something glowed jack-o'-lantern orange. Her first thought was: *fire!* She smelled no smoke, though. When the hay around her began to undulate, she scrambled for the barn door.

She was screaming. Ashley was screaming.

She could hear the camera crunching under the hay like an aluminum can. She leapt over the threshold, into the yard, and landed face-first onto the grass. It was oddly slimy, sticky, like someone had lathered it in Vaseline.

She squirmed to her hands and knees as something swished through the air over her back. Ashley let out a wet, shrill cry.

A pitchfork had lodged itself into Ashley's lower abdomen. The tines were sunk all the way into her belly. Blood blossomed across the bottom of her shirt and the crotch of her pants like an angry rose. More of the crimson liquid spewed from between her lips, dribbling down her chin. The pitchfork twisted clockwise, shredding shirt and flesh, bringing forth another desperate scream from Ashley. This one sounded more like a high-pitched gargling.

Carson found her feet and rushed to her friend's side. Her analytical side tried to make sense of what had occurred. The pitchfork had flown; therefore, someone must have thrown it. But she could've sworn the barn was empty. And how the hell had the tool twisted on its own?

Her mind ran through these questions in a matter of milliseconds. All the while, Ashley coughed and gagged and twitched.

The pitchfork twisted again, this time rending itself free, pulling back toward the barn door and twirling a length of guts like gory spaghetti. Carson attempted to catch Ashley as the young woman was pulled by her tangled innards and the pitchfork toward whoever—whatever—had thrown the object.

Carson looked and wished she hadn't. The hay covering the floor of the barn had risen into an amorphous mass of tendrils and bulges surrounding a bright orange orifice that could only be some type of maw. Teeth like ridged daggers lined its edges, and the throat beyond pulsated with red-orange light.

Several of the tendrils had taken hold of Ashley and the pitchfork and were dragging her on her knees into the opening. Ashley had been reduced to a bloody, blubbery mess. Her arms twitched like beheaded snakes. More straw-bundled limbs engulfed her the deeper she went into the barn. Bones cracked as the monstrosity constricted her prone, dying body. By the time she reached the creature's infernal mouth, Ashley was a broken doll of meat and bone. The dregs of her life force manifested only by a final series of pathetic whimpers before the mouth of the hay beast closed over her head, shoulders, and chest.

Carson ran from the nightmarish scene. In her panic, she ran away from the barn but also away from her new house and her car. She ran past the cornfield and into the dark woods.

***

Regis drove onto the historic covered bridge over Tucker County Creek. Shooter Jennings on the stereo barely drowned out the creaking of the boards under the weight of his car. Though he knew the bridge was safe, he still held his breath whenever he crossed it—a ritual left over from childhood. Once he reached the other side, he headed north on Route 473.

The road was mostly even, despite the occasional dip. Exhaustion from a full day, but mostly from attending to his father, weighed down his shoulders and head. He kept his hands tight on the wheel and tried singing along to keep himself awake.

He slapped himself on the cheek. Turned the music up louder. Took the curve by the old feed mill with extra care.

He blinked hard and took another curve. Reminded himself there was a stop sign coming up.

The song changed to "Me and the Whiskey" by Whitey Morgan and the 78s, another good track. He clenched one fist and rapped it against the steering wheel to the beat.

Just a little longer and then he'd be home.

When he reached the stop sign, his thoughts wandered. To the Barnyard Days Festival. To Phil. To his father.

Then further back. To that night. To Lydia. Her grandparents' barn, not far from here. What he'd seen or thought he'd seen.

He stepped on the gas with extra force in hopes of driving away from what haunted him but knowing damn well that he couldn't.

As he rounded another bend, someone ran into the middle of the road. His foot found the brake again. This time, he slammed on it and jolted in his seat.

The young woman stopped running and faced his vehicle. Awash in the headlights, he could see every troubling detail. She was covered in dirt and debris. She was breathing heavily, perhaps hyperventilating. Her eyes were pulled wide with something between bewilderment and terror. She gritted her teeth, and he thought he saw something like blood between her lips.

Regis got out of the car. He held up a disarming hand, but he kept his other hand near his holster just in case. He didn't expect she would pose a threat, but if someone was after her, he wanted to make sure he could defend them both.

"Ma'am," he said, taking a cautious step forward. "It's okay. I'm with the Sheriff's Department. Can you tell me what happened?"

She just stared at him. Kept taking laborious breaths through her teeth. Her face was as white as a sun-bleached skull.

"Ma'am?"

The young woman collapsed in the middle of the street.

Chapter 7

When the scar on Lydia West's forearm began to itch, she worried she had accidentally cut herself. It was a long way from the cutting board and the assorted veggies to her left forearm, but she had certainly been distracted enough. Seven-year-old Roger was snatching the stuffed T-Rex from two-year-old Annabelle, causing his little sister to wail at the injustice. Lydia took a breath, readying herself to admonish the boy again, but instead, the old, reaggravated wound drew her attention.

The scar, white for nearly two decades, now shone an angry pink and was darkening by the second. The longer she stared, the more the old wound seemed to change, to pulsate, like something beneath her skin wanted to burst through. Pink deepened to red. Red to maroon. The skin around the scar began to swell. Crimson and purple splotches bloomed over the bloated flesh like fireworks. Itch became inflammation.

Roger cried out, and for a second, she was brought back to that night in the barn. The night little Alvin …

Roger stamped his feet as he entered the kitchen. The intrusion ripped her gaze from her warping, throbbing limb. Roger's face was red, and fat tears rolled down his cheeks. The sight and sound of him rendered pain and memory into distant echoes.

"Annabelle scratched me," he cried.

Lydia exhaled and glanced back down at her forearm. The scar had returned to the twisty white ridge she took great care to ignore on most days. The pain was gone now, but the memory of that night lingered close to the surface of her consciousness, threatening to pull her into a state she'd spent years fighting hard to avoid falling into.

"Let me see," she said and held out her hand.

Roger started to compose himself, taking deep breaths and wiping away tears. In the adjacent living room, Annabelle was hugging the T-Rex to her chest and pacing innocently. Roger showed his mother the top side of his hand.

A pink mark glowered up at them between his middle and ring fingers. Annabelle hadn't broken the skin.

"You're okay. See, no blood."

Roger nodded and said, "Okay."

"She shouldn't have scratched you, but she's still little and still learning. You can't be antagonizing her like that."

He nodded again. "Okay."

She led him into the living room, where Annabelle was still walking back and forth, holding the stuffed pink dinosaur. Lydia knelt in front of her and said the little girl's name. Annabelle didn't look up, but she didn't try to get around her mother or walk the opposite way.

"Annie," she said in a gentle voice. Annabelle kept her face cast toward the unicorn shoes on her tiny feet. "We don't scratch. Can you say sorry to your big brother?"

"No!" Annabelle hollered.

The sudden sharpness and increased volume of her toddler's voice made her shoulder and neck get tense. This often happened when she experienced loud, unexpected noises or found herself in an environment of overstimulation. A doctor had once told her it was a symptom of post-traumatic stress disorder.

If they only knew...

"Annie," Lydia said again. She still tried to keep her tone level and soft, but she could feel the waver in her voice, the frustration simmering underneath. "It isn't nice to scratch someone, even if you're upset with them."

Annabelle kept her head down. She seemed completely shut down. This happened sometimes, usually after an altercation with someone. Lydia worried about this. Sometimes, she lay awake wondering if something crucial was missing from her daughter's emotional makeup. As if she lacked the ability to feel remorse.

"Annie, will you please apologize to Roger?"

The front door opened with a thump. Braeden's heavy footsteps drew everyone's attention. Annabelle's face brightened, and she ran with arms outstretched toward her father, saying "Da-da! Da-da! Look, it's Da-da!"

"Hey, sweetie," he said, bending to wrap Annabelle in a hug.

"Hi, Dad," Roger said. The seven-year-old had found his tablet, the confrontation with his baby sister now forgotten.

"Hey, buddy-boy, how's it going?" He lifted Annabelle, and she clung to him like a koala to a tree. His brow furrowed when his gaze landed on his wife. "What's wrong?"

"We had an incident," Lydia said with a sigh.

"Uh-oh." He was still smiling when he said it. He had a nice smile, immediately disarming, even after years of familiarity with it.

Her limbs relaxed, but she tried to keep her expression stern. "Annabelle scratched her big brother."

He held Annabelle enough so he could meet her gaze. "Now, why'd you go and do a silly thing like that?"

"I was teasing her," Roger said without looking up. "I kept taking the T-Rex away."

"He was antagonizing her," Lydia said. "But that's no excuse …"

"You're right. Annie. Can you say sorry to Roger?"

"Sorry, Roger!" she said, all her r's like w's. Lydia found it adorable, even now.

"It's okay, Annie," Roger said, still fixated on his game.

"Do you want to say something to your sister?" Lydia said.

"Sorry, Annie."

"See," Braeden said. "Easy fix."

"Yeah. Nothing to it." Lydia huffed and turned back toward the kitchen. She heard Braeden set down Annabelle and follow her. When she reached the cutting board, she faced her husband and tried a smile. "Thank you for your help."

He raised his eyebrows. "Everything okay?"

She thought about watching her scar changing shape. For a second, she considered telling him about it.

Bad idea, though. He loved her and knew her better than anyone else did, but he didn't know all the details of what happened that night twenty years ago. No way could she tell him she might be ... might be what? Crazy? Having flashbacks?

Behind him, Annabelle had joined Roger on the loveseat and watched him play his tablet.

She shook her head. "I just wish he wouldn't mess with her all the time."

Braeden shrugged one shoulder. "What are big brothers for?"

Lydia's guts clenched like someone had taken them in a tight fist. Heat flared in her cheeks and forehead, and her pulse quickened to a throb.

"Lydia?" Braeden said.

"I'm sorry. Can you finish chopping veggies? I need to lie down for a bit."

"Sure, let me just wash my hands."

She pushed away from the counter and made for the bedroom at a brisk pace. Inside, she shut the door and turned to the full-length mirror. She stared at her reflection, not seeing the woman she had become. Instead, she saw a teenage girl. A kid.

The same kid who couldn't protect her family.

The same kid who led her own flesh and blood to a horrific death.

Chapter 8

The young woman from the road stirred in the passenger seat. She whimpered and glanced around her new surroundings. Her gaze met Regis, and she stared at him. Undeniable trauma swam in her eyes like undulating storm clouds. Regis had seen the look before. In paranoid vagrants. In teenagers on too much psylocibin. In car accident victims.

"You're safe now," he said. Her expression did not change. "I'm Sheriff of Tucker County. Can you tell me what happened tonight?"

She looked away, facing the darkness of the tree-lined road. She wrung her hands, twisting her fingers until he thought they might snap. He faced the road and tried to think of something more to say. Licked his lips and flexed his hands on the wheel.

"What's your name?" he asked.

The darkness and trees gave way to scattered porch lights and lamp posts of the Reaper's Bend suburbs. He slowed to match the speed limit. Some of the houses had fallen into disrepair. Awnings sagged over cluttered porches. Chipped siding and hail-damaged roofs gave the impression of insufficient shelter. But there were other homes, ones in much better condition. Luxuriant colonials and brick-fronted, single-family fortresses existed alongside the dying structures. They seemed to exist despite their less fortunate neighbors or, perhaps, even because of them.

"Carson," the woman said.

"Carson? Who's that?"

"Me."

"That's your name?" He thought that was a boy's name but decided not to mention it. She nodded once, her head like a heavy weight on her neck. "Are you hurt, Carson?"

She looked at him again. Her gaze still held that haunted look. She didn't appear wounded, at least not physically.

Regis pulled up to the station for the second time that night. Outside, Phillip and Avery were waiting to assist.

Regis cut the engine. "Can you walk?"

Her answer came in the form of a single nod, which he returned before going out to open the door for her. He held out his arms to help her up if she needed it, but she rose on her own. He stepped aside to give her some room to walk. As she passed him, her head moved as if on a swivel, like she expected an attack.

Phillip gave Avery a nudge. "Well, get the door for the lady."

The new deputy headed dutifully toward the door. Carson beat him to it and flashed him a look that told him exactly how she felt about needing a door held for her. Avery shrugged at Phillip and headed in after the young lady. Phillip laughed at his trainee's minor misadventure.

"I could tell she was one of those independent types," Phillip said. "I just wanted to see that look right there on the rookie's face."

Now it was Regis's turn to glare.

"Sorry, chief. Just trying to lighten the mood."

"Some moods aren't meant for lightening," Regis said.

Phillip swallowed the last of his laughter. "She say what happened to her?"

"She's barely said a thing."

Inside, Daisy had already risen from her desk to help Avery take Carson to the interviewing area.

"Come on, through here," she said. She put one gentle hand on the small of Carson's back and the other on her elbow. "Can I get you anything, dear?"

Carson shook her head once, like it was a heavy thing.

"Are you sure she doesn't need an ambulance?" Daisy asked, now addressing Regis. "She looks like she's suffered quite a shock."

"Shock doesn't even begin to cover it," the young woman said. Her voice sounded rough and ragged. Avery's eyes twitched at the woman's sudden speech.

"Hey, she speaks," Phillip said with a slight chuckle.

"Give it a rest, Phillip," Daisy said.

"Avery," Regis said. The new guy squared his shoulders. "You don't need to jump to attention. Just stay with Daisy and the young lady, see if they need anything. If she starts talking or anything changes in her condition, you let me know." He nodded at Phillip. "I want you on the radio. Get any available units checking the area where I found her."

"What are you gonna do? Go home?"

Regis shook his head. "No, I'm going to get some coffee because I have a feeling it's going to be a long night."

Chapter 9

Lydia couldn't sleep, so she lay in the dark and prayed none of the amorphous objects moving about in the surrounding shadows became fully realized. A bandage now covered her forearm. She could no longer stand to look at the scar there. Even in the dark, she feared it would be too visible, as if it might start to glow with stirring hellfire if she didn't cover it. The bandage only served to make her perpetually aware of its presence, and this barrier didn't keep away the dark memories that kept her conscious.

"Go upstairs to your room," Grandma said. "You're gonna be fine."

"But Alvin's dead!"

"That's right." Grandpa Al reached for the door. "You just remember that when I go out there and put a bullet in him. He's not your brother anymore."

"And it's my fault," Lydia whimpered.

Grandma attempted another hug. "There, there. You didn't know any better."

But that wasn't true. Lydia had known the stories.

She simply hadn't believed them.

Something hammered on the door, making its hinges rattle. Lydia flinched, but Grandma stood still like she was carved from stone. Grandpa Al took a step back and flexed his hands on the rifle. A gurgling bellow from outside followed the blow on the door.

"Go," he said through gritted teeth.

Something beat against the door again. Hard enough to sound like a gunshot. Another bloodcurdling cry followed.

"*No, I'm staying right here,*" *Lydia said.*

"*She'll need to see this eventually, dear,*" *Grandma said.*

Another bang against the door. Another wet shriek.

Grandpa Al's face sagged as if he was about to cry. "*He's her brother. Our grandson!*"

"*Not anymore. Just like you said. I'll mourn for the boy once that monster stops wearing his skin. If she wants to watch, she can watch.*"

And watch Lydia had. Watched and witnessed what couldn't be unwitnessed. Couldn't be forgotten, not entirely. Even between triggers, a latent but simmering terror lay under the surface. Close enough to breach at will.

Grandpa Al bit his lip and nodded. He unlocked the door and gripped the knob. "*Everybody stand back.*"

He turned the knob, and Alvin spilled inside. The boy still had the goat's head mounted onto his fist. Red and gray brain juice covered his forearm like a liquid sleeve as he held the macabre puppet high. The animal's legs remained lodged in his torso and backside, the blood-drenched furry appendages twitching with hideous life.

He swung the goat's head wildly, and Grandma pulled Lydia out of striking distance. He screamed again, and the goat screamed with him. Both their eyes blazed with orange fire.

Grandpa Al took aim, but another swing of the goat's head knocked him off-balance. He stumbled down to one knee. He winced as he tried to regain his stance, arthritis and wooziness conspiring to keep him kneeling and prone.

Alvin raised the goat head high. The boy swung it down in a fierce arc, burying the curved horns into his grandfather's skull.

The impact tore Grandpa Al's forehead asunder with a wet crunch, soaking the last wisps of white hair he had with blood and brain matter.

The gore slopped its way down his face, seeping into his glazed eyeballs and into his gaping mouth. It spattered his bedtime slippers, joined by piss that soaked through his pajama bottoms and dripped sour-smelling dots onto the rustic hardwood.

Lydia could not stop screaming.

She wanted to scream now, but she knew from experience that a scream would only provide temporary relief. It had provided none on that awful night.

As she screamed herself raw, Grandma released her and calmly walked to where the rifle had dropped. Alvin yanked the goat's head out of Grandpa Al's skull, causing more blood and brain goo to spurt from the wound as Grandpa Al collapsed into a puddle of his own evacuated fluids.

Alvin turned to Grandma and bared his teeth. Black bile drooled from his shredded lips. Grandma pointed the rifle at his face and fired. The impact dropped him to his back. A bloody entry wound smoked at the center of his face.

Without missing a beat, Grandma stepped on Alvin's wrist to pin the screaming goat's head and fired another shot. The horned head burst apart from getting hit at such close range. Hunks of brain and shards of skull sprayed the surrounding floor and soiled the frilly hem of Grandma's nightgown.

She pressed the muzzle against Alvin's chest and fired a third shot into his corrupted heart. His body jerked once and fell still. When she pulled the rifle away, Lydia saw the bloody hole the shot made. The ruined remains of his heart still jumped with animation. Blood was spurting from severed arteries, and something was wriggling in the mess. To Lydia, it looked like a cluster of worms. Or a tuft of grass caught in an underwater current.

The smoke filling the air did nothing to mask the stench of death. Grandma faced Lydia. Beads of sweat glistened on the elderly woman's forehead, but her eyes gleamed with frightening youthfulness. It dawned on Lydia that somehow Grandma found this whole horrifying ordeal exhilarating, even with her grandson and lifelong husband now lying dead.

Lydia rolled to her side and crammed a pillow between her knees. She pinched her eyes shut, knowing she wouldn't fall asleep unless she relaxed but still wanting to show the universe she was trying. On the other half of the bed, Braeden gently snored, oblivious and at peace. He slept like a man without ghosts—or at least like someone whose ghosts didn't scream.

Lydia stopped screaming, but only out of sheer exhaustion. She opened her mouth to speak, but no words would emerge.

"Pull yourself together," Grandma said, setting the rifle against the wall by the door. "We've got some secrets to keep tonight."

Beneath the bandage, her scar began itching again. The blanket shifted as Braeden's shape bent into a ninety-degree angle. He now sat beside her. His figure loomed over her, deeply shadowed. A smell of sunbaked grass radiated off him, a stark contrast to his usual scents of coffee and Old Spice.

"Braeden?" Lydia whispered.

His eyelids lifted to reveal eyes clouded over with orange light like twin fiery pools. She scooted away from him, pushing aside the pillow and shimmying out of the comforter. Her feet slapped against the hardwood floor. She hoped getting out of bed would ground her, awaken her, but the nightmare continued. This was no dream—it was a vision.

Braeden's lips parted slowly, like opening a lid from an ancient coffin, but instead of rusty hinges creaking, something gritty emanated from the expanding jaws. In the back of his throat, the orange light from his eyes flickered like candleflame. The hellish glow revealed a tongue replaced with a braided tendril of wet weeds. The new appendage lolled out and ran across his chin, leaving a dark residue.

"We need to bring a sacrifice, she said." The voice was dual toned. A low-pitched growl was layered over a chirpy little boy's voice. The demonic voice disturbed her less than the tone that was unmistakably little Alvin's. "She didn't know she was bringing us two."

The dual tones broke into a warped cackle. Hot breath blew against Lydia's face, smelling like charred flesh. She stumbled backwards, and her right ankle rolled. With a sharp cry, she collapsed. Her elbow and hip struck the floor and she spat out a half-uttered curse.

Her husband stepped out of bed and loomed over her, a broad-shouldered shadow person, no longer the man she loved.

"*No!*" she yelped, writhing on the floor, trying and failing to find her feet.

Braeden's heavy hand gripped her shoulder. "Lydia," he said in the same two-toned voice.

She thrashed her arms and kicked. Shrieked like an animal in a rusty trap. His free hand found her other shoulder and gripped it. He peered into her face, his eyes full of swirling magma, his mouth clogged with black tendrils.

"Lydia," he said in his own voice. And just like that, his face became the one she knew, the one she kissed on their wedding day and nearly every day since. "Lydia, you're okay. You were dreaming."

She shook her head. "No, I wasn't."

"You were," he said, sounding like he meant to convince himself as much as he wanted to convince her. "You were."

She glared up at him, examining his face for any anomalies. Though the room was still dark, she could tell his face was his own. She recognized the high cheekbones and strong jaws. The full lips ringed by five o'clock shadow. His eyes no longer held that orange flare. This was her husband, the man who fathered her children and had shared a bed with her for nearly a dozen years.

She nodded too quickly. "You're right."

He held her gaze for several more seconds. He then nodded much slower than she had. His hands found hers and pulled her to her feet. "You didn't hurt yourself, did you?"

"I'm sure I'll bruise, but I didn't break anything, if that's what you mean."

He kept her hands in his and maintained eye contact. More seconds passed with them standing in the dark holding each other. "Do you want to tell me what that was about?"

"I don't remember," she said, the lie coming too easily.

He didn't let her go, and for a second, she expected his face to change again. Imagined him becoming one of that demon's agents and dragging her screaming back to the barn. Into the mouth of hell.

He released her and said, "Okay. Let's go back to bed."

She nodded again, this time trying to do it slowly to project a return to normalcy. "Give me a minute."

Lydia shuffled off to the adjacent bathroom while her husband crawled back to his side of the bed and cocooned himself in the comforter. She closed the door and switched on the light. Temporary blindness accosted her, and she closed her eyes while they adjusted. In the mirror, she saw a woman with dark circles around her eyes and thinning hair that fell in anxious tangles.

With a sigh, she opened the shuttered medicine cabinet and brought out a bottle of Ambien. She popped one pill, shut off the light, and stomped back to bed. This time, the darkness took her, and it was mercifully shapeless.

Chapter 10

"It's about two young women who move into an apartment haunted by the victims of Jeffrey Epstein," Deputy Judith Cane said.

Her partner, Deputy Roy Patrick, side-eyed her from the driver's seat. Roy was a former Army Ranger and tended to remind people of androids from movies about dystopian futures. A stark contrast to Judith, who currently had a full pot of coffee churning through her bloodstream.

"Sounds trashy, I know, and believe me, it is, but, like, I dunno, I kinda liked it," she said.

Roy took the cruiser down the Big Hill Road and turned onto Route 473. "And what did you say it was called?"

"*The Scary of Sixty-First.*"

"That's not grammatically correct. It's missing a noun."

"At least it has some hot lesbian action."

Another side-eyed look. "I'm not a lesbian."

"Maybe not, but every straight guy likes to watch."

He didn't have a response to that. Not a spoken one, anyway. He flexed his hands on the wheel and licked his lips. Judith took that sign of slight discomfort as a victory.

"I don't even know what we're doing out here," she said.

"We're on the lookout for anything out of the ordinary."

"Nothing weird in Reaper's Bend. No, sir."

Roy eased his foot off the gas pedal, bringing the vehicle to a slow crawl. His jaw clenched and unclenched, an almost imperceptible movement beneath his hard features. The engine quieted to a hum as they came to a stop at an unmarked trailhead leading into the wooded grounds of Henshaw State Park. Judith's gaze followed Roy's as he scanned the dense forest. The trees seemed to bend toward the cruiser, their branches reaching out like gnarled, beckoning fingers.

Her bubbly demeanor switched to cop mode. She lowered her window and reached for the spotlight attached to her side mirror, flipping it on to cast a bright beam into the dark woods. Straining her eyes, she spotted a sleek body amidst the thick foliage—a car parked in the shadows.

"Did you see that from the road?" she asked.

"Headlight reflected off it," he said and switched on the light bar so anyone zipping down the dark road would see them and slow down.

Judith reached for the radio. "Cane here. We're off Big Hill Road near the Bypass. We've got an abandoned vehicle parked up an unmarked nature trail. Patrick and I are checking it out, over."

"That's a copy," said a voice that wasn't Daisy's.

"Lee, what are you doing working radio?" Judith asked. Roy pointed to his eyes and gestured toward the car in the woods. Judith sighed. "Never mind. We'll report back. Over."

"Ten-four," Phillip Lee said.

The deputies stepped out of the cruiser and closed the doors. Crisp night air enveloped them like a blanket stuffed with ice packs. Out here, the smell of pine needles and dead leaves hung thick and oppressive. The chirping of countless crickets was an incessant wall of sound. Grass and nature's detritus rustled under their footsteps as they stepped onto the trail, shining their flashlights into the shadows.

"What do you think happened out here, anyway?" Judith asked.

"Maybe we'll find out. Maybe we won't."

"It must have been bad. I heard that girl fainted."

He made a sound of agreement in his throat.

When they reached the Toyota Camry, she continued shining her light around the vicinity while Roy shined his inside the vehicle's windows. Other than the crickets, the woods had other sounds, but none drew her immediate attention. The rustling to her right was too small to be a threat. The snap of a twig came from too far away. Those croaking sounds, only toads.

She walked around the car with uneasy confidence, telling herself this discovery was a clue at best and an unrelated abandoned vehicle at worst.

"Anything inside?" she asked over her shoulder.

"Lots. Looks like someone's living in it."

"It doesn't look like the kind of car a bum would drive around. It's too nice. At least on the outside."

Roy grunted and bent down to look under the car. Judith pointed her flashlight up the trail. The beam splashed illumination on a dark human outline standing over a dozen paces ahead.

"Um, Roy?"

Roy looked up from the car and stood up straight when he spotted the figure in the middle of the path. "You there, identify yourself."

The figure took a step forward.

"I don't like this," Judith said.

"No," Roy said, unsnapping his holster. "Not at all."

The broad-chested figure stalked forward, his long strides cutting through the shadows. Judith's flashlight shone in his face, but he kept coming. As he closed the distance, she could tell there was something wrong with his face, but she couldn't put her finger on it.

"That's far enough," she hollered.

He didn't stop coming. He moved like a wind-up toy made of flesh and bone, full-sized and with plenty of time to burn on his clockwork motor. Twigs snapped and gravel shifted under each steady footfall. He was dressed in an untucked flannel shirt, faded denim pants, and one muddy cowboy boot. His other foot was bare and filthy with wet grass and dead leaves.

The closer he came, the more Judith's insides recoiled. Her hand found the holster of her weapon. She flexed her fingers around it.

"Don't take another step," Roy said.

The figure kept coming.

"What's wrong with him?" Judith whispered.

"Drugs," Roy said. "That's what's wrong."

Judith took a good look at the man's face. His eyes held an orange tint that spread across the whites and the irises. Even the pupils seemed affected, though that might have been some trick of the light. His mouth leaked a dark fluid that reminded her of engine oil. Something was moving under his shirt, causing it to bulge and ripple.

"I don't think so," she said.

As the distance continued to close, Judith became aware of a rank odor coming from the man. He smelled like a compost heap of dead grass and food scraps in various stages of decay.

He was nearly upon them now. He was unarmed, but his fingers kept flexing and relaxing. It could've just been a tick, but Judith wondered if he was preparing to do something.

Roy released the grip of his gun and stepped forward. He held out both hands and placed them on the man's shoulders. The man kept trying to come, but Roy held him at bay. The man's feet dragged, kicking up dirt and leaves as he tried to proceed forward.

"Take it easy now," Roy said, meeting the man's washed-out gaze. "What's going on tonight?"

The belly section of the man's shirt stretched outward. It looked like he had another arm under there. Or a ball python.

"Careful, Roy," Judith said.

Roy glanced back at her, quickly but not fast enough.

One of the man's hands snapped into action. Reached between Roy's arms and grabbed onto the deputy's face. His index and middle fingers tunneled into Roy's right eye, causing it to pop like an overripe berry. His thumb jabbed into the roof of Roy's mouth as ocular goo spilled over his hand. He gave a hard yank, and a sickening sound, part wet crack and part ripping fabric, echoed through the air.

Roy flailed and spun on his heel, giving Judith a full view of his face's ruination. His skull now bore a jagged hole that joined his nasal cavity and eye socket. Flaps of torn flesh wavered around it like flags in a light breeze. His attempts to scream sent blood burbling up from his throat. It was the cry of a man drowning in his own gore. He fell jerking into a cluster of leaves, the dry ones rising in the air as if attempting to flee this scene of macabre violence.

Judith ripped her gun from its holster and aimed for the sick motherfucker's heart. No word of warning, no attempt at nonlethal force for this asshole. He'd just killed her partner of six years, a father of four, the only man whose company she could tolerate for more than ten minutes. She had never shot anyone in her entire career and often lay awake nights hoping such a scenario would never present itself. But now, she squeezed the trigger, fully intending not just to shoot a man but to kill him. To kill him out of sheer rage because that was all this savage murderer deserved.

She fired three times. Each bullet buried itself in the man's chest and filled the air with an accompanying concussive blast. Each shot should have been a fatal one, a fact confirmed when the man fell to his back and didn't move.

She breathed rapidly, raggedly. Her hands trembled. Her entire body trembled. Her vision liquefied with tears.

"Motherfucker," she whimpered. Then, she screamed it: "*MOTHERFUCKER!*"

The dead man sat up. Judith's flesh went cold. The chill pierced its way inward, turning her blood to ice water. The man staggered to his feet, giving her a view of the bullet wounds. Each hole leaked more of that dark fluid. Something wriggled inside. She'd dropped her flashlight when she drew her gun, so she couldn't quite make out what was causing the movement, but it looked like worms.

She raised her weapon again and trained her sights on the bastard's head. Something moved to his right, rustling dead leaves and bending a low-hanging branch with a creak. Her gaze flicked toward the sound. She gasped in disbelief and knelt to snatch up her flashlight to confirm what she saw.

Roy was also rising back to his feet, slow and shambling, like a child rising from sleep his body demanded but his mind denied.

"Roy, don't get up," Judith said because she could think of nothing else. "I'll get you some help."

Roy faced her and killed what little hope her sanity clung to. His remaining eye now held that orange haze. Something pulsed and squirmed within the crimson crater the man had dug into his face. More worms, she thought, but they looked like strands of straw.

She pointed both gun and flashlight from one man to the other. Her arms shook violently now, like someone pressed a cattle prod to the base of her skull.

Judith turned and ran toward the cruiser. The shotgun was inside. She could radio for backup. She could drive the hell out of here and never look back.

She sprinted past the abandoned Camry. Leapt over protruding roots and stones. The flashlight beam jumped up and down with every bounding step. Though she kept up with her cardio, the onset of panic quickened and shortened her breath. Her heart felt like it was lodged between her ears and about to explode.

She ran with such speed, propelled by so much frantic energy, that she ran thighs-first into the cruiser and nearly somersaulted over the hood. She caught herself, losing both gun and flashlight in the process. The strobes from the light bar bathed her in red and blue, their centrifugal motion seemingly timed to her accelerated pulse.

She scrambled to the passenger door and jerked it open.

The cruiser wasn't empty. A woman sat in the passenger seat. She looked like she should be dead, but she wasn't. Her midsection was torn open and stuffed with hay. Blood ringed her mouth and nose. Myriad punctures lined her arms, each of them holding a single strand of hay. Her body had undergone all this serious trauma. Yet, the eyes were aglow with an eerie golden light, and she was holding the shotgun.

Judith went to shut the door again, but the figure inside the cruiser muscled her way out, leaving a gooey puddle on the seat. Judith stumbled backwards. Before she could regain her balance, the woman from the police car rammed the butt of the shotgun into her chin.

The impact snapped her jaw off one of its hinges and took her off her feet completely. As she fell, she could taste her own blood and feel loose teeth rolling across her palette like a mouthful of pebbles. She coughed and choked as the disemboweled woman stepped to her side and bent down.

Judith's head swam with panic. She felt frantically around the dirt for the gun, the flashlight, a stone. Her hand found no purchase before her attacker dropped a knee across her chest, stealing her breath. Even with the wind now knocked out of her, she thrashed in hopes of freeing herself.

She might as well have been under an anvil.

The woman who had been waiting in the cruiser—a vessel of flesh once belonging to one Ashley Casey—reached into her shredded abdomen and pulled out a fistful of bloody hay.

Judith gargled out a final protest through the blood and dislodged teeth before the disemboweled woman buried a fist into her mouth, knocking out the rest of her front teeth and stuffing her throat with straw.

Chapter 11

"After that, I ran through the woods," Carson said. "I guess I was so panicked I must have gotten turned around. I wound up in the middle of the road, and Sheriff Regis brought me here."

Carson looked up at the other faces in the room. Daisy sat closest to her. The elderly woman had a softness in her eyes. She projected a level of compassion that had made it easy for Carson to talk, even coaxing out the more unbelievable details of the account. Pieces of the story that Carson herself had a hard time believing, even as she relayed them.

Regis was doing everything to appear neutral and mostly pulling it off. Only the briefest of glances, exchanged with Daisy, clued Carson in that something else was up. The room, with its plain white walls and artificial lighting, held a palpable tension that heated her skin.

"What are you not telling me?" Carson asked.

Her gaze flicked to the young deputy, Avery. He was slack-jawed and staring inward. She guessed he didn't believe her. Probably thought she was nuts.

Regis licked his lips. "Thank you for being so forthcoming. Are you sure you don't need any medical attention?"

"You mean like a shrink?" Carson asked with some acidity.

Regis spoke slowly. "You've been through something traumatic, and I want to make sure you're given the proper care."

She held his gaze for a beat, then shook her head. "No, I don't need a doctor. I just want to go home. I want to sleep, though I don't think I'll be able to."

"Can I call someone for you?" Daisy asked, still maintaining her grandmotherly demeanor. "Maybe your parents?"

Carson patted her pockets and looked herself over. "Fuck. I don't have my phone. Or any numbers memorized."

Regis and Daisy exchanged another glance. Avery stared at a blank spot on the wall. The deputy was barely older than her, and she got the impression that he wanted to be anywhere else. An idea occurred to her. "Is there a computer I can use?"

"Huh?" Regis said.

"A computer. I can check my social media and see if anyone is able to come get me."

Regis looked to Daisy for guidance.

"She can use mine," she said. She extended a hand for Carson. "Come on, dear. Can I call you dear?"

Carson stood on her own. "Sure, though I'd prefer your majesty."

Regis stayed by the interview room door while Daisy got Carson set up at the computer station.

"Need me to relieve Phil?" Daisy asked.

Phillip looked at Regis expectantly.

"Not yet. I want to talk with you and Avery first."

Avery, who was halfway out the interview room, did an awkward twirl before heading back inside.

Phillip grimaced and muttered something under his breath.

"What was that, Deputy?" Regis gave Phillip a look to remind the deputy that he'd meant what he said earlier about taking him out back and smacking him around if he was insubordinate.

"Nothing, sir."

"Great. Any word from the units patrolling the area where I found her?"

"Judith and Roy found an abandoned vehicle and were going to investigate."

"About how long ago?"

"Ten minutes, give or take. I just radioed for an update but haven't heard back."

Regis looked at Carson. Her face had gone several shades darker. "Keep me updated," he told Phillip.

He followed Daisy into the interview room and closed the door. He stood with his back to it while Daisy and Avery stood on opposite sides of the room's only table. On paper, he was the man in charge, but right now, he didn't feel like it.

"So, what do we think?" he asked.

"I dunno," Avery said.

"I know you're in training," Regis said, "but you've got to be thinking something."

"Her story sounds like there's devil shit going on. Either that, or she's crazy."

"Crazy," Regis repeated. Memories threatened to surface. Memories of one night nearly twenty years ago. He shook his head, hoping to dissipate them like a cloud of steam. They lingered, though, dormant monstrosities beneath the unfathomable sea of his consciousness. He nodded at Daisy. "What do you think?"

A rare darkness shaded her features. It sent a sharp chill through Regis like someone had injected ice water into the place where his skull met his spine. She said, "Are you sure you want him to hear what I'm about to say?"

Avery crossed his arms as if to shield himself from a stiff breeze. Regis considered Daisy's question and then asked one of his own. "You from around here, rookie?"

"Yes, sir."

Daisy rubbed her fingers together and clenched her jaw. She stared expectantly at Regis as he mulled over his next decision. As small as Reaper's Bend was, Regis couldn't honestly say he knew everyone in town. He decided to take Avery at his word.

"Whatever you're about to say, I'm sure he's heard in some form or another."

"Well, okay," Daisy said. "If what that young lady said happened anywhere other than the West barn, I'm not sure I would've bought it for a second. But that place plays by different rules."

"Because the Wests were devil worshippers, right?" Avery said.

At this, Daisy's brow creased. "I used to see Al and Maggie West in church every Sunday. I don't think it was a question of who they worshipped. As far as I know, they were good Christians. But well, desperation can make people do crazy things, like compromise their values."

"They made a deal," Avery said, his voice wavering with uncertainty like he was a kid answering a question in a classroom.

"To keep their crops growing in abundance," Daisy said. "And truth be told, the whole town benefited."

"It's why we have the Barnyard Days Festival," Regis said through gritted teeth.

Avery's eyes widened. "That's why you hate it so much."

"I don't know why, in the twenty-first century, we're still celebrating lame superstitions."

"But it's a lot more than that, isn't it?" Daisy said.

The dark memories again began to stir within the shadows of his mind. Soon, they would crawl into the light of recollection, living nightmares he hoped to never face again.

"You know your ... father ... had a part in it," Daisy said.

He nodded, and as if this acknowledgment was all it needed, the mental horror show began to play.

Chapter 12

The phone blared, pulling Regis away from the game of Unreal Tournament. *The temporary distraction was enough for his opponent to blow his character to bits with a flak cannon. Red filled the screen, and a flash of text asked if he wanted to continue. The phone rang again. It was the line in his room, the one Lydia always called. Excitement blossomed in his chest, obscuring the disappointment of losing another campaign.*

He pushed away from his desk and grabbed the phone off his nightstand. "Hello?"

"Regis?" Usually, he loved the way Lydia spoke his name, but he didn't like the way she sounded now, not one bit.

"What's wrong?"

She told him, and he listened. He was a good listener—at least that was what Lydia always told him, and he usually believed what she and others told him. He was the kind of person who took others at face value. But what little he could make out between her sobs simply defied belief. Even though, like everyone else in Reaper's Bend, he had heard all the eerie rumors about her grandparents and their land many times before.

"Okay," he said. "Okay, okay. Let me ... I'm going to send you some help. Just, uh, sit tight."

He hated how unsure of himself he sounded. How childish.

"Hurry," she whimpered and disconnected the call.

Regis took the handset from his ear and stared at it. For several seconds, he couldn't move at all. He could only try to comprehend the ridiculous but admittedly frightening story Lydia had relayed to him. Regardless of the more outlandish details, his girlfriend was clearly in trouble. He slammed the phone back onto the cradle and left his bedroom.

Downstairs, he found his father posted up in front of the television. Onscreen, Sting suplexed The Great Muta off the turnbuckle of a wrestling ring.

"Dad," Regis said in a wavery voice.

Abram Jones blinked, sat up straight, and looked at his son. When he saw the boy's expression, worry creased his face and he stood. "Regis, what is it?"

"It ... it's Lydia. She's in trouble."

"Lydia?" His expression turned severe. "That West girl? I told you not to see her anymore."

"I know, Dad, but just listen—"

"Don't tell me to listen, I'm your father. That family is nothing but trouble."

Sting tossed Muta into the corner and jumped on him. The announcer called the move a Stinger splash. The crowd went wild on contact.

"That's what I'm trying to tell you," Regis said. "Something's happening over there. She said ... she said something came out of the barn and ... killed her brother."

Abram's eyes widened. He stood up arrow straight and marched to the coat closet where he kept his belt and gun. Regis watched as his father strapped the belt over his sweatpants before grabbing his badge and keys from the ceramic bowl on the entry table and opening the front door.

"Dad?" Regis said.

Abram turned and faced Regis. A thousand-yard stare glazed over Abram's deep brown eyes. Regis had never seen his father like this.

"Stay put," Abram said.

"What? No, I'm going with you."

"No, you're not, boy. Girlfriend or not, this is police business now." He stepped outside and shut the door with a concussive thud.

Regis stood there shaking, staring at the closed door as his father's vehicle rumbled to life. Regis shook his head and headed for the back door. Outside, he trudged through the overgrown lawn until he reached his bike. He mounted the Schwinn and pedaled like he had hellhounds on his trail ...

... not knowing that hell was just where he was headed.

He would be headed there again tonight, this time having traded two wheels for four and empty hands for a Glock.

"Now wait," Avery said. "Just because I'm familiar with the stories doesn't mean I believe them."

Daisy opened her mouth to argue, but Regis held up a hand. "No one's asking you to believe anything. But the fact is that young lady said something happened at the Barn on the Wests' property. She says someone's been killed. I say it's our duty to check it out."

"Of course," Avery said.

The meeting adjourned, and Avery left the room first. Daisy caught Regis by the wrist on his way out. "You gonna be all right?"

"I'd like to think I'll be a lot better when I find out what happened tonight, but I don't think I will."

"You don't need to go. You're the Sheriff. You can delegate."

"You know me better than to suggest something like that."

She gave him a stern gaze that was more matronly than grandmotherly. After a beat, she nodded. "You're right." She looked away and chewed her bottom lip. When she faced him again, her expression had softened. "Your father is a good man. He just got caught up in—"

"You don't have to explain anything."

She pressed her lips together. "Right."

Chapter 13

While Regis and the others discussed her statement, Carson scrolled over and over through the list of her online friends. She kept hoping someone else would become available, someone close by who could help her. Mayber her parents or someone who could contact them.

Anyone but Jennie Silva.

The deputy working the radio—Phil, she'd heard him called—kept glancing over at her, thinking he was being subtle about it. He was not.

"Fucked-up night, huh?" he said.

The inquiry made her grind her molars. "Uh-huh," she said.

She did not have the patience for casual conversation. She kept seeing that pitchfork twirl its way out of Ashley's belly, taking a string of guts with it. And all that hay roiling like some textured golden sea.

She must have hallucinated it. At least some of it?

Ashley was dead, though.

Impaled. Devoured by all that straw.

And it wasn't exactly Jennie's fault—it was Carson's.

"No one awake?" Phil asked.

She blinked at the second intrusion. She pressed her lips together and shook her head.

"That's okay," he continued. He held up the radio's mouthpiece. "No one awake out there either, it seems."

"Aren't you worried?" she said.

He gave a half-shrug. "Too old to worry."

"Must be nice," she snipped.

She couldn't accept that Jennie fucking Silva was the only person she could call for a ride. Carson would almost rather ride in a cop car again, but she'd had more than her fill of police talk tonight. Even if she hadn't, Regis and the others probably had plenty to do already.

It was either Jennie Silva or a cab.

This sucks.

She hovered the cursor over Jennie's profile thumbnail and blew out a long breath. Resigned to the fact that it was her only option, she clicked on Jennie's heavily filtered face to open a chat and began typing her message.

When she finished, she hesitated over clicking send. The door to the interview room swung open again and stole her attention. Phillip turned around too as Regis and the others entered the lobby.

"Did you find a lift?" Regis asked.

"Uh ... I think so." She clicked send, trying not to make a show of it. "I'm just waiting for a response."

"Good. Let me know." His brow deepened as he paused for a moment. "Okay, Avery. Phil. Let's drive out to Al West's barn and look around."

Phillip pushed away from the desk like he couldn't get away fast enough. Daisy was there to meet him.

"Thanks for keeping my seat warm," she said.

"Anything for you, doll," Phillip replied with a wink.

Daisy sat down and gave a subtle eye roll that only Carson seemed to catch. Carson smirked at the sentiment shared with her, and Daisy winked.

The messenger app made a pinging sound.

"That your ride?" Regis asked.

Carson checked. It was a single-worded response from Jennie Silva. *Sure*, it said. Nothing to indicate concern for Carson's well-being, just a short response that all but told Carson that Jennie would do it, though she wouldn't be happy about it. To be fair, Carson hadn't mentioned Ashley's death. She had, however, said she was at the Sheriff's Office and something bad had happened.

Carson hoped she wouldn't take too long to arrive.

"Everything good?" Avery asked.

No, everything was not good. What a ridiculous question.

Regis put a firm hand on the young deputy's shoulder and squeezed. "What my colleague meant to ask was, 'is you're ride coming?'"

"Yes, she is," Carson said. She maintained eye contact with Avery. "Thanks for asking."

"Ma'am," Avery said and gave a slight nod.

He headed toward the back where Phillip was getting a coat on. There was a shiftiness to the way he walked, and she wondered if it might be his first night on the job.

"I'll meet you guys in the parking lot," Regis said, heading for the door.

"I'll hold down the fort," Daisy said. "Be careful out there, Sheriff."

Chapter 14

As he pulled onto the gravel drive at the edge of the West property, Regis felt the sort of numbness that only came when trying not to think about something.

He tried not to think about coming here all those summers ago with Lydia.

He tried not to think about all those times spent holding her hand while they sat on the thickest nearby tree.

He tried not to think about running through the surrounding woods in the rain the day she kissed him for the first time, his back pressed to the side of the barn, laughing as the rain soaked them.

The last thing he could afford to do was let his mind wander to more innocent times.

After weaving through a maze of thick trees and grassy fields, he pulled to a stop in front of the West residence. The house was a collapsing mirror image of its former self. One corner of the foundation was sunk into the earth as if being slowly devoured, while its roof was shedding shingles like snakeskin. Dirty cracked windows clouded the view of the inside.

The cruiser carrying Phillip and Avery rolled to a stop beside him. Regis got out, and the other deputies followed. He and Phillip left their vehicles running, the headlights splashing illumination over the house and the barn beyond. The moon hung overhead like a spectral spotlight in the black sky.

"Stay alert, gents," Regis said in a level tone.

The front door to the West house groaned open. A gaunt, hunched figure was standing in its frame, leaning on a cane.

"It's Magdalena West," Phillip said.

"I thought she was dead," Avery whispered.

The old lady limped onto the porch and coughed. "Not yet, to some people's chagrin, I'm sure."

"Ms. West. It's Regis. Sheriff Jones. These are my deputies. Phillip Lee and Avery Joel."

"Regis?" She laughed and it sounded like sandpaper on wet concrete. "What brings you out here?"

"It's not a social call, I'm afraid."

She stepped into the light. Even from several paces away, the sunken eyes and sagging jowls stood out in stark detail. She appeared every bit as broken-down as her home. Instinct and experience told him this was more than simply the toll of years gone by—something was draining her life.

"How can I help you then, Sheriff?" She smiled and revealed teeth gone to rot.

Avery swallowed and flexed his hand around his flashlight.

"I've got a woman at the substation," Regis said. "She says something happened out here tonight."

"Something's always happening, isn't it?" she said.

Regis stepped forward. "Not just anything, I'm afraid. Otherwise, we wouldn't be out here."

"She said someone's been killed," Phillip said. "It supposedly happened on your property."

She raised her bristly white eyebrows. "Is that so?"

"Did you see or hear anything tonight?" Regis asked. "Anything out of the ordinary?"

"Well, a couple girls came sniffing around here 'bout two hours ago. I think one of em just moved into the house on the other side of that hill." She pointed a crooked finger between the deputies. Regis followed the gesture and saw a hill covered in tufts of long grass. "I told them to look around if they wanted. They said they were curious about the barn."

"What'd you tell them?" Phillip asked.

"Not much. Just that they were welcome to look around."

"You don't mind if we look around, do you?" Regis asked.

Magdalena shrugged. "You can do whatever you want. You're the Sheriff. Not sure you'll find anything, though."

Regis considered her words and the meaning behind them. She used to be so nice to him. Now, she struck him as cold and conniving. Not someone he could trust. "And you're sure you didn't see or hear anything after you saw the young ladies?"

"Can't say that I did, but I'll tell you the same thing I told them. Look around all you like. Got nothing to hide. People around here know everything there is to know about me."

"Thank you, ma'am," Avery said.

Regis and Phillip looked at him. Regis faced Magdalena again. "We'll let you know when we're done. If you think of anything in the meantime, let us know."

"Will do, Sheriff," she said and punctuated her statement with another black-toothed grin.

They watched as she slowly turned and hobbled back inside. The door clicked shut behind her. The house remained dark, and Regis wondered how she managed to get around without falling and breaking her hip.

"Man, that must have been awkward, her being the grandmother of your old girlfriend and all," Phillip said with an underlying smugness in his voice.

"She gives me the creeps," Avery said. "And I think she's lying."

Regis gestured to the barn. "Let's check it out."

The men passed along the side of the house. Grass rustled against their pant legs. Regis could feel something moist on the blades through the fabric, but the air was dry.

"Anyone else smell that?" Avery said.

Regis wrinkled his nose. "It'd be hard not to."

"Rumor has it she uses a special kind of fertilizer," Phillip said. "It has some, let's say, infernal origins."

Regis swallowed. "Let's not worry about any rumors tonight."

More memories from that night threatened to surface. He focused on taking one step at a time. Hoped grounding himself would keep the nightmares at bay. Even as he was headed to the source of them. Even as he walked the same path Magdalena and his father had used to carry the bodies from the house to the barn.

First, they'd taken a larger form—Lydia's grandfather. A smaller form was taken next—little Alvin. He'd watched them close the barn door and something reddish orange glow through the seams in the wood.

It wasn't real, he told himself, knowing damn well it was.

"Hey, come look at this," Phillip said.

"Yeah, what's up?"

"Looks like some devil shit," Avery said.

He was standing behind Phillip, shining his light on the barn door's edge. His eyes held something like the expression a kid might have as he asked one of his parents to check the closet for monsters.

Regis looked to where Avery was pointing his flashlight. Someone had burned a strange symbol on the door, only ... Regis shined his own light at the adjacent edge of the wall. The other half of the symbol had been carved there too.

"It's like opening the door breaks the seal," Avery said.

"Is that your professional opinion, rookie?" Phillip asked.

Regis knelt down to examine the symbol more closely. "Assuming it is a seal, I'd say the rookie isn't too far off. The question is—"

"What was it keeping inside?" Avery said. Regis and Phillip looked at him. He held up his hands and forced out a laugh. "I mean, hypothetically."

Regis cast another look at the halved symbol. It was made mostly of severely drawn lines and several points. Between each point were etchings that easily could've been smaller renditions of the larger symbol, intended to give the illusion of an eternally repeating pattern.

"Yeah," Regis exhaled. "Hypothetically."

Again, he thought of that night. Wondered how much had been real. Wondered what, if anything, he should tell Avery and Phillip.

"You know what I don't see?" Phillip said.

Regis stood and looked around. He even peeked into the crack made by the door standing ajar.

"Any bodies," he said.

"Bingo."

"Why would she lie?" Avery asked.

"I'm not saying she did," Regis said. He pointed his flashlight into the barn. "We still haven't looked inside."

"You believe her, don't you?" Phillip said. He shook his head and coughed out a chuckle. "You know your daddy used to come out here a lot the past twenty years." Regis glared at him. "Maybe the original Sheriff Blazing Saddles and Maggie West were having a little fling. Or maybe everything people say about this place is true, and he was helping her make sacrifices."

Regis aimed his flashlight directly at the deputy's eyes. "You listen here and listen good. If you don't shut up about my father right fucking now, I'm going to kneecap your racist ass with this flashlight."

Phillip held up his hands in a *don't shoot* gesture, but he had a shit-eating grin plastered across his face. "Sorry, Sheriff. Just spit balling."

"Are we really going in?" Avery asked.

"Rookie, are you sure this job's for you?" Phillip said.

"Easy, Phillip. Yes, Avery. We're really going in. There's three of us, and we're armed. I wouldn't worry."

Regis stepped into the barn, and hay crunched beneath his booted foot. Phillip and Avery followed. The inside of the barn looked largely undisturbed. Immediately visible were several hills of hay, some scattered old tools, and a gray, wooden wagon wheel. The darkness of the hour made the place more shadowed, full of dark corners Regis could only examine fully when he shined his flashlight.

"I don't like how quiet it is," Avery said.

"Let me guess," Phillip said. "You're gonna say it's 'too quiet.'"

"Well, now that you mention it, yeah! Yeah, I am."

"Keep it down, fellas," Regis said. He shined his light under the loft, then up at the rafters. "Hm."

"No victim, no crime." Phillip switched off his flashlight and placed it back in his belt.

"I'm not ready to give up that easily. We may need to get forensics out here. And a team to search the grounds when we have daylight working in our favor."

"We should probably check the loft," Avery said in a shaky voice.

"Mighty brave of you to volunteer yourself, rookie. Go on ahead."

"Actually, Phillip, why don't you show him how it's done. Lead by example."

"I can do it. You're right. There's no reason to be spooked. That ..." Avery paused, choosing his words wisely. "Carson's story can't be true. And the symbol on the door, that's just graffiti. Nothing to be afraid of. Besides," he held up his sidearm, "a little satanism is no match for a good old nine-millimeter."

Phillip clapped Avery on the back. "That's the spirit, kid."

He began to climb the ladder. The rungs creaked under his weight, but he breathed easy and moved deliberately.

The radio crackled, and Daisy's voice came through too garbled to understand. The sudden burst of static jolted Avery and nearly made him lose his footing. He wobbled and wrapped his arms around the nearest rung like a toddler clinging to his mother's neck.

Regis gritted his teeth. "Can you repeat that, Daisy? We got a bad connection."

She tried again, but the signal still came through scrambled. Regis looked at Phillip to see if he'd gotten any of that.

"Didn't catch it." Phillip's mouth twisted into a smirk. "My hearing's not what it used to be."

Up on the ladder, Avery was still hugging one of the rungs.

"You need me to go up there instead?" Regis asked.

Avery shook his head a little too rapidly.

"Okay, well, I'm going to go outside and see if I can get a better connection. And Phillip? Don't give him a hard time."

"Wouldn't dream of it, Sheriff."

He said it in a way that was meant to get under Regis's skin, but Regis didn't take the bait. He headed for the door while Avery resumed climbing to the loft, albeit at a slower pace.

***

"Regis, are you there?" Daisy said and groaned when he didn't immediately answer.

Upon first meeting the woman, Carson couldn't imagine her getting this flustered. Sure, it could happen to anyone, but Daisy had a down-home sweetness about her that reminded Carson of a kindly old schoolteacher or librarian. Now, Daisy's brow was pinched with a frustrated determination as the radio squawked static at her.

Carson was curled up on one of the chairs in the waiting area. It was the opposite of being comfortable, even with her sweater bunched up to create a barrier between her back and the chair's arm. She just wanted to sleep, but that wasn't going to happen until she got in her bed, and maybe not even then.

"Regis, we've got a problem. Over."

Another hiss of static. A seething breath from Daisy.

"Daisy, can you hear me?"

Daisy sighed at the sound of the sheriff's voice, but her relief was short-lived. "Regis, I still can't raise Judith and Roy. Units are checking the area, but they're coming up empty-handed."

"Shit," came the response from the radio.

"You're telling me. Where the hell could they be?"

Something banged on the window beside Carson's head.

She yelped and nearly jumped completely out of her seat. Daisy glared past her at the offending knocker. "Is that a friend of yours?"

Carson spun to see Jennie Silva standing outside, waving and grinning like this was all some fun night on the town.

"Yeah, that's my ride. Sorry."

"Well, have her come in a minute."

"Daisy?" Regis asked on the radio.

"Hold on a minute." Daisy reached over to buzz Jennie in.

As Jennie approached, another figure met her at the door.

Chapter 15

"Daisy, did you copy that?" Regis asked on the radio.

He released the talk button and waited for a response. When none came, he sighed and took a few more steps away from the barn. Even though he could still feel the buzz of caffeine in his veins, his body wanted nothing more than to lie down. Every step felt heavy, and he could feel a headache coming on. He'd had just about enough of tonight. While he was glad to do his best to protect and serve his community, he found himself wishing he'd never run into Carson on his way home.

He held down the button to try hailing Daisy again, but the sound of Phillip screaming from inside the barn cut him off.

"Regis, get me out of here!" Phillip hollered. "There's ... something in the hay."

Regis had a passing notion that Phillip might be fucking with him. On any other night, he wouldn't put it past the bastard, but now, there was something in the elder deputy's voice that suggested this was anything but a prank.

"Regis, please!" He banged on the barn door.

Regis approached to find the door now shut. Perplexed because he hadn't heard it close, he gave the handle a firm pull, but it wouldn't open. The chain containing the padlock lay at his feet, partially obscured by a tuft of grass and faded from years in the sun. The door could only be latched from inside.

"Is it locked on your side?" Regis asked.

He barely heard himself over Phillip ramming his shoulder against the opposite side. "It's alive ... the hay is alive!"

"Phil? What's happening in there, buddy?"

"Regis! I'm ... so fucking sorry. I've been an asshole." He was nearly blubbering now.

Regis pulled his firearm and took a step back to aim. "Phillip. I need you to stop talking like that, and I need you to get away from the door if you can."

"O-okay," he sputtered.

"Let me know when you're clear."

"I'm ... oh, Jesus! I'm clear. I'm clear!"

Regis fired several shots into the door, all around the latch area. When he finished shooting, there were five smoking holes in the surrounding wooden planks. At this range, they were considerable, and they leaked a liquid the color of dark garbage bags. Under the pounding reverberations from the reports, there was another sound, a furious peal that reminded him of a siren but strangely organic like the scream of a dying whale.

"Phillip?" he said, though he had the bizarre notion that the cry was coming from the barn itself. The dark fluid continued to leak from the holes in time with a pulsing that vibrated through the red-painted planks. "Phillip!"

The door burst open, nearly smacking Regis in the face, but he stumbled backwards in the nick of time. Phillip stood front and center, as surprised by the opening of the door as Regis. His face was twisted and pale, unbelieving and utterly terrified by the events of the past few moments.

Behind him, Regis saw the cause for the deputy's fear. The hay did indeed appear to be alive. It had risen like an amorphous hill, undulating with massive gasps of husky breath and, beneath that, the glow of something yellow and bright. The tangled strands at its base held the broken form of Avery Joel. He wore a blood-ringed smile on his boyish features and his eyes held no life.

Phillip barreled toward Regis like a twenty-year-old track star and not an older, overweight officer. But his urgent strides weren't fast enough.

One of the straw tendrils lashed from the base of the hill and found its target. The strands of hay pierced through the seat of Phillip's pants, ripping first through fabric and then through flesh. Phillip lifted off the ground as the limb tunneled between his glutes and into his bowels.

Regis continued to back away but couldn't bring himself to turn and run. He tried to strategize a way to get Phillip down, to help somehow, even as the limb went deeper through Phillip's insides.

Part of Regis simply didn't believe his eyes. The stress of the job, coupled with caring for his alcoholic father, must have caught up with him, causing his mind to snap. Though he was aware enough to know this was no dream, he thought perhaps that he was no longer seeing things the way they were. His damaged psyche had distorted his senses, making him see monsters after hearing Carson's bizarre story.

The charred, rancid odor grounded him firmly in the horrific present, completely and dreadfully aware of what was occurring in front of him.

Phillip spat blood as he tried to scream. He held out his twitching arms and hung cruciform in midair. Places on his abdomen bulged as the offending intruder continued working its way through him.

Regis wanted to shoot, but he couldn't make up his mind what to shoot at. He also didn't believe his bullets would do anything to harm this entity. The rounds shot into the barn door had only seemed to anger it.

In the churning madness, Avery's corpse sank deeper into the hay, limbs breaking further and one eye popping from his head. Regis was nearly hypnotized as he watched it dangle from a blood-slicked optic nerve.

The loud crack of Phillip's breastbone drew Regis's attention back to the dying elder deputy. Something tumorous protruded from between Phillip's pectorals, warping the bulletproof vest and stretching the fabric of his shirt until the buttons popped off. More blood waterfalled down his chin, not just coming from his mouth but now his nose as well.

This was no hallucination. It was too fucking real.

Something whistled through the air, and he dropped to his butt. The landing was painful and sent a whoosh of air from his lungs. As he hit the ground, he saw some projectile sail overhead.

He shimmied backwards, struggling to his feet as the tendril snaked its way up Phillip's gullet with a sound like shredding, wet bedsheets.

Phillip vomited out the straw limb. For a moment of indeterminate time, it jutted out like a grotesquely oversized tongue. Phillip's eyes rolled to the whites, and his arms fell limp to his sides. The tongue split into smaller twists of hay that bent back like fingers to cage Phillip's head.

The tendril retracted and took Phillip with it into the barn.

Regis found his feet and bolted for his cruiser. He came upon Magdalena West, pinned to a rotting stump by the wagon wheel. It had entered her torso longways and buried itself in her sternum and abdomen. Her ribcage had split open, the individual ribs tangling with the rotted spokes. Offal spilled over the wood, vomiting onto her lap and splattering her shoes.

Regis continued his retreat, thinking how it very well could've been him the wagon wheel impaled, but he took no moment for gratitude as he barreled for his cruiser. He reached his vehicle and quickly closed himself inside. He set his weapon on the passenger seat and grabbed for the radio as he reversed.

"Daisy, are you there? I'm in deep shit out here."

He cut the wheel and accelerated up the gravel drive, back toward the road. In the rearview mirror, the glow inside the barn had turned fiery orange. The straw tentacles thrashed at the air outside the wide-open door.

The radio crackled and Daisy said, "We're in deep shit over here too!"

Chapter 16

The lady in the deputy uniform smashed Jennie Silva's pretty face into the glass door of the sheriff's office until her face was no longer pretty. Jennie went limp and began to slide down the glass. Fractures now split the pane, and each crack sliced a new gill in Jennie's cheek. By the time she reached her knees, Jennie had left a snail trail of blood following her to the bottom half of the door.

The uniformed woman kicked the glass, splintering it the rest of the way. Shards plinked and clattered to the floor as she stepped through the new opening. Jennie fell forward, impaling her chest on the jagged edges of the pane. She reached out a bloody hand toward Carson and Daisy.

"Help," she gurgled. "Please."

Almost as an afterthought, the uniformed woman turned around and lifted her booted foot.

"Judith, don't!" Daisy yelled.

The boot came down, and Jennie's head burst apart, spilling its contents across the linoleum. The boot came back up, dripping bloody hunks of fat and gore. A hairy flap of scalp clung to its treads.

Carson gagged and something acidic burned her esophagus. She put her hand to her mouth and swallowed her gorge. She didn't have time to puke.

Judith faced them and took a step forward, scraping the filth from her boot. Carson could see now that bundles of hay were stuffed in Judith's shirt at the cuffs and chest. Smaller strands of hay dangled from her cheeks and throat, wriggling like parasites sucking at her pores. Yellow fire filled her eyes. She opened her bloody mouth and emitted a sound so high and screeching that Carson and Daisy both needed to cover their ears.

When she finished screaming, Judith grinned with muddy teeth. Her eyes had dimmed, but the faint light still flickered in the recesses of her pupils. She reached for the nightstick on her belt. Someone gripped Carson's wrist.

Carson jerked free and faced whoever grabbed her. Even seeing that it was Daisy brought no relief. Carson kept looking back at the smashed skull of Jennie and the uniformed woman who'd done the smashing.

"We need to go," Daisy said in a harsh whisper.

It was then that Regis called again, telling Daisy he was in deep shit out by the barn. Daisy swiped up the radio and pressed the talk button. "We're in deep shit over here too!"

With that, she tossed the radio down and forced Carson to follow her away from the front desk. Behind them, Regis radioed that he was on his way. Judith lurched after them with a deliberate, frightening confidence, clutching the nightstick in a bloody fist.

They ran toward the hall leading to the emergency exit, holding hands like a couple of scared kids navigating a funhouse on Halloween night. They were nearly across the lobby when something smacked Carson on the side of the head, dropping her to the floor.

The blow made her woozy and filled her mouth with a metallic taste. She blinked and, through blurred vision, saw Judith continue approaching, sans nightstick. Carson struggled to sit up. Daisy was gone, running the opposite way. Leaving her.

"Where are you going?" she tried to yell but could only whine.

Judith was only five feet from her now. The deputy's hands now made claws instead of fists. Dirt and straw clung to the fingernails as if she'd recently dug a hole with her bare hands. The nail on her right ring finger had been mostly snapped off and now hung by a sliver. The yellow glow in her eyes brightened to liquid fire that filled even the whites.

Carson staggered to her feet as Judith fell upon her. She tried to scream, but the hand with the hangnail took her by the throat, reducing her cry to a meager wet croak. Daisy was nowhere to be found. The old bitch had left her to die.

Judith lifted Carson and put her back against the wall. Carson tried to pry the fingers from her neck. She kicked and squirmed, but the seemingly possessed woman held fast. As Judith squeezed, Carson's vision darkened and swam. The fight began to drain from her limbs.

Dying. I'm dying. What a terrible fucking day.

Terror and pain overtook all cognitions. She felt the intense blind panic known to animals in the talons or jaws of a predator. Black and red slashed across her vision. Even weakened, a second surge of resistance set her limbs into a thrashing frenzy. Judith reared back her free hand to claw off Carson's face.

Then, Carson was released. As she fell, she inhaled. A sonic concussion followed her descent. She seemed to fall farther than she remembered the floor being, as if the ground had given way, spilling her into some black abyss.

The smell of a spent shotgun shell brought her back to the surface of consciousness.

She lay in a crumpled mess against the wall. Beside her, Judith lay in a heap with half her face reduced to a red and black smoldering hole. Down the hallway, Daisy pointed a smoking shotgun at the fallen Judith with hands that trembled.

"Ohmygodohmygod!" Carson scrambled to her feet and nearly collapsed.

"Take it easy," Daisy said. The older woman was next to her now, shotgun lowered, helping Carson to stand. "No one gets up from that."

Carson looked again at Judith's body to confirm this was true. The deputy lay silent and still, the blood leaking from her face the only movement. Carson nodded through tears and doubled her efforts to stand. Laughter burst from her lips, and she threw her arms around Daisy's neck in a show of hysterical gratitude.

"Okay, okay," Daisy said, patting Carson on the back. "I'm gonna get on that radio and call for backup from the other substations, maybe the State Police. EMS can come take ... Judith ... away."

"Why did one of your deputies try to kill us?"

"I have a feeling that's not Judith Cane anymore," Daisy said as she ushered Carson back to the front desk.

"God, my head hurts," Carson said, putting her fingers to where the nightstick grazed her. "I feel like I got hit by a truck."

"We'll have EMS look at you too, if you'd like."

Carson rubbed the sensitive area. "How much is that gonna cost me?"

"They can send me the bill."

Carson smiled at her, even though she was sure that wasn't how medical billing worked. Daisy started to smile back, but then her eyes went wide. The expression made Carson's heart plummet. Even though every instinct told her not to, she looked behind her.

Judith had sat up. She looked their way with her now ruined face. It was still smoking, still bleeding, but she just grinned with her remaining teeth through the gory mess like this was all in fun and the damage was merely the result of good special effects. Strands of hay writhed within the gaping wound like emaciated maggots.

"Oh God!" Carson shrieked.

Daisy pushed her aside and picked the shotgun back up. Judith stood as Daisy racked another shell. Daisy leveled the weapon at Judith's chest. Before Daisy could fire, the deputy went low for a tackle. She attempted to readjust her aim, but Judith scooped the backs of both of Daisy's legs, dropping her hard on her back.

Judith snatched the shotgun from the fallen woman.

Without thinking, Carson grabbed the nearby computer keyboard, yanking it out of its USB port and holding it like a Louisville Slugger. She charged and swung.

Judith caught her by the elbow with one hand and hurled her across the room. Carson tumbled several feet, only stopping when she collided with the wall. She tried to get up again, but this time, she was too banged up. Pain and exhaustion weighed her down like she had cinderblocks affixed to each limb.

Judith jabbed the shotgun into Daisy's chest like a stake into the heart of a vampire. The breastbone crunched from the impact and blood fountained from around the entry point.

Judith held on to the gun, jerking it back and forth like a lever. The motion crunched more bones in Daisy's torso. Made a grotesque squishing sound as organs ruptured. More bodily fluids spattered from the wound, soaking Daisy's clothes and making scarlet puddles on the surrounding floor.

Daisy's arms flailed, but these were the final impulses of a body that didn't know the meaning of death; they were futile efforts to hold on as Daisy puked and spat out the remnants of her life force.

Judith stood and took a moment to watch as Daisy made a bloody mockery of a snow angel. Her own wound knitted together with the help of the living straw, transforming the ghastly hole into a twisted scar.

Carson shimmied to her feet, using the wall for support. Judith stepped toward her; she was inevitability incarnate. Carson barreled down the hallway, toward the emergency exit, on legs that threatened to buckle, with Judith only a few paces behind.

Something heavy crashed into the wall, followed by several reports that ripped through the station. Carson spun to see Judith slumping against the wall. New holes in her torso wept dark fluid.

Carson frantically scanned the rest of the station. Her gaze landed on the newcomer and relief ignited in her chest. "Regis! Oh, God."

She ran into the sheriff's arms. Tried blubbering out an explanation but could only manage hysterical gibberish. He squeezed her tightly, then let go.

"Daisy," he said, and he strode to the older woman's side. Dropped to his knees. "Daisy, I'm so sorry."

The shotgun stuck out of Daisy's ruined chest cavity like a flagpole. Regis touched it and withdrew his hand. Looked in Daisy's eyes, at the face twisted in a final expression of pain and terror, and had to look away. He turned toward Jennie's headless form and then looked at Carson. His face crinkled with a maelstrom of mixed emotions. "What happened?"

Carson shook her head. "I ..." She wiped her eyes. "I don't know."

Regis looked back down at Daisy. His mouth tightened like the expression of a man swallowing something bitter. "I do. Dear God, I think I do."

Chapter 17

The phone buzzed on the nightstand, hoisting Lydia out of a dead sleep. The room was still dark, but mercifully, the blackness held no shape. Still groggy from the Ambien, she checked the number. She didn't recognize it, but seeing the area code woke her up like a cold hand striking her cheek.

"Hello?" she said.

"Lydia, it's Regis."

She flung off the comforter and swung her feet to the floor. Behind her, Braeden gasped awake. "What time is it?"

She covered the phone's mouthpiece. "Late. Go back to bed. I'm just ... using the bathroom."

She strode out of the bedroom and shut the door before uncovering the phone. "Regis? Is it really you, or ...?"

She didn't know how to finish that sentence.

"It's me," he said. "I'm sorry if I woke you, but—"

"Something's happened at my grandparents' barn, hasn't it?"

A long pause. "How did you know?"

"Never mind," she said. "What's happened?"

"Jesus Christ. What *hasn't* happened would be a more appropriate question."

"That bad?"

"I've lost four deputies tonight, and Daisy ... she's dead."

Her heart clenched, and she squeezed the phone. "Oh, Regis, I'm sorry."

Another, longer pause. "It's not your fault."

What are big sisters for?

She swallowed. "What can I do?"

"Can you help me seal it back inside? Do you know how?"

"My grandmother might. Have you asked her?"

"Lydia, your grandmother's dead too." He waited for her to respond.

"God rot that fucking bitch," she said.

"Her and your grandfather, they really made some kind of deal, didn't they?"

"Yes."

"Can you help?"

"I ... maybe."

"Maybe?"

"I mean, I don't know. There was this page in the contract."

"The one they made with the devil?"

"Yes, that one. Are you going to tell me you don't believe in that sort of thing?"

"Shit, after what I've seen tonight ..."

"That's what I thought. Now, I remember a certain clause that would void the whole thing."

"So we wouldn't need to seal it in the barn and pray it doesn't get out."

"That's the idea."

"How soon can you get here?"

"I can get there by morning."

"Fuck. Okay. In the meantime, I'll set up a perimeter. Make sure no one gets near that barn. It's just that tomorrow is ..."

"Barnyard Days," Lydia said.

"Yeah."

"Shit. Okay, I'll hurry."

"Great. And, Lydia?"

"Yeah?"

"I know you're married now, and you've got a family, but I wish I was seeing you again under better circumstances."

"Me too," she said. "I'm on my way."

She disconnected and set down her phone. She looked at the bandage on her forearm. As if it detected her gaze, orange light in the shape of her scar pulsated under the dressing.

"Where are you going, Mama?"

Lydia flinched and turned toward the inquirer. Roger was standing on the stairs, watching her with eyes that seemed so fragile, so innocent in the darkness of the house. She forced a smile. "Just a drive, sweetheart. But Mama will be back in a few hours."

"Why do you have to leave in the middle of the night?"

"I just need to take care of something. Come on, I'll walk you back to bed." She followed Roger up the stairs and tucked him in. Gave him a kiss on the forehead and headed back downstairs.

She wrote a note in a hasty scrawl that said *NEEDED TO GO HOME. I'LL EXPLAIN WHEN I GET BACK*. Stuck the note under the *Paw Patrol* magnet on the fridge and grabbed the keys to the Subaru from the hook by the front door.

Before stepping outside, she scanned the interior of her house.

"I'll be back," she said, ignoring the voice in her head telling her she would never see this place again.

Chapter 18

Orange sunlight sliced its way up from the horizon as Lydia passed the sign for Reaper's Bend. The scythe-wielding farmer carved into the wood welcomed her with his familiar toothy grin. She drove in silence, the noise in her head providing enough din as she mentally walked through what she had to do. Her phone lay in the cupholder beside her, dark and silent; any minute now, Braeden would wake up and see her note and call for an explanation.

The trees, their branches thinning with the arrival of autumn, lined the road like skeletal sentries. She knew this drive well. Every curve she took and every pothole the vehicle bumped over felt like an encounter with an old friend.

An old friend who harbored the desire to destroy her.

She flexed her hands on the wheel and drove on, bracing herself for more brushes with the sinister familiar.

***

Regis pulled into the driveway of his dad's place. The crooked shutters and chipped siding sent a sting to his chest. The house was falling apart. Would continue to fall apart. Just like his father.

He cut the engine and headed to the front door. Exhaustion pulled at every limb, bone-deep and heavy, rendered his attempt at a purposeful stride into a lazy shuffle.

It had been one hell of a night, and the day would likely prove no less arduous.

He knocked hard and waited for an answer. Jabbed the doorbell and tried not to pace. When Abram didn't come to the door, Regis fished out his key and let himself in.

The smells of beer and garbage greeted him like bad hosts. Over the years, he'd grown used to these roommates of his old man, but today, he had no patience for them.

"Dad!" he yelled.

No answer.

He made his way to the bedroom, where he found Abram tangled in a sheet and snoring. A beer can that hadn't been there last night when he put his father to bed now sat on the nightstand. The TV was dark.

Regis gritted his teeth. "Dad."

Abram moaned and rolled over but did not rouse. A high-pitched fart trumpeted from between his butt cheeks.

Regis stepped over the discarded comforter and grabbed Abram by the shoulder. He shook hard enough to make Abram's head wobble. "Dad, wake up."

With a moan, the former Sheriff twisted to life. He threw a wild haymaker, clipping his son on the chin. Regis staggered backward, bracing himself on his right leg and holding his balance. The blow stung, more from surprise than the force of it.

Abram sat up and blinked several times. "Regis? How'd you get in here?"

Regis held up the key, which prompted a nod from Abram. "I need your help."

"Couldn't it wait until morning?"

"It's morning now." Regis pressed his lips together and exhaled out his nose. "Dad, it's about the barn."

Abram's eyes widened. His mouth moved but made no words.

Regis continued, "I need to know everything you know about the thing that lives in it. How do you stop it? Can you kill it?"

Abram looked to the side and grabbed the beer can off the nightstand. It still had some liquid in it. "I don't know what you're talking about."

Abram raised the can to his lips. Regis snatched it away. "Cut the shit, Dad. I lost five people last night. One of them was Daisy."

Abram's eyes went dark. "Daisy's dead?"

"Yes. She's dead because one of my deputies got infected and turned into a bloodthirsty killer."

"Daisy's dead." His voice came out scratchy and strained.

"You can stop pretending I didn't see you and Magdalena West feed the bodies of Lydia's brother and grandfather to that thing. I was watching from the cornfield, and I know you saw me because I saw your fucking face."

Now Abram stood. "You have no idea what you're on about, boy. Everything I did as Sheriff was for our town. To keep it safe. To keep you and your mother safe."

"You helped Magdalena keep it fed, didn't you? And not just the one time."

Abram's expression was all the answer he needed.

"Jesus, Dad."

Abram sagged back onto the bed. "If you don't feed it and feed it right, then you risk it getting out."

"Well, it's out now. What do I do?"

Abram stared at the wall like he was peering into the barrel of a shotgun. His torso inflated like an oversized balloon with every troubled breath.

"Dad?"

Abram didn't look at him. "You should go."

Regis's phone vibrated in his pocket. Lydia's name on the caller ID. He gave his father a final look, then stomped out of the room, leaving his father to rot.

***

Carson opened her eyes in a strange place. She sat up and worked backwards in her mind to figure out where she was and how she'd gotten here. Recollection hit her like a right cross from a heavyweight. Her stomach clinched and her gorge threatened to rise as she remembered Ashley's twisting guts, Jennie's spilling brains, Daisy's cracking sternum.

She remembered Regis telling her she couldn't go home. He needed his deputies to check the area because her new house was too close to the West place. Too close to what happened.

He sent her to a motel in Reaper's Bend, a place called Shady Elm, while he filled out a report, notified next of kin, and coordinated the logistics of guarding a perimeter around the West property. The glamorous side of policework, he'd called it, flashing a grim smile that told her none of it was glamorous in the least.

He'd given her a phone and told her to wait for him to text her with an all-clear. She sat up and checked it.

No texts. No missed calls.

She opened the rideshare app and hailed a ride home.

Chapter 19

Lydia stood outside the wreckage of the Sheriff's station. Through yellow tape on the destroyed window, she could see dried blood on the floor and black bullet holes in the wall. The deputy working the front desk once manned by Daisy Keener had a gray, wasted look to him, like he had seen what happened here—or at least the immediate aftereffects of it. He hardly noticed Lydia was there. He only kept watching the phone on the desk as if begging it not to ring.

When Regis pulled up, something surprising rose in her chest. It was surprising given the circumstances and the passage of time but there nonetheless. It was a wave of nostalgia, of longing.

This was the first man she'd loved, though he was too young to be a man at the time and she'd only been a girl herself. She steeled herself as he opened the door, but then their gazes met, and twenty years dispersed in an instant.

They embraced, and she looked at him, as if to confirm he was truly there.

"I know how I look," he said, pulling away but keeping his hands on her elbows.

"Please. You've aged a lot better than me."

"I wouldn't say that." He glanced to the side. "Thank you for coming."

She released him and stepped back. "I didn't come back for you. I came back—"

"To finish it, I know."

"Right. Yeah." Now she looked away and back. "Think I can borrow a gun?"

"You're not planning on going back to that house alone?"

"Yes, I am. This is my fight."

"No, it isn't. I'm going with you."

"This is my family we're talking about. Their curse."

"Well, I'm the sheriff."

"So, you're giving me an order? Is that it?" She got close to him again, this time with no warmth. "I don't work for you."

"But you need someone to cover you while you look for that page." Something twinkled in his eyes. "Besides, if I'm giving you a gun, that makes you my deputy."

"You enjoyed saying that, didn't you?"

"Maybe a little." His face went serious. He reached down and unstrapped a small revolver from an ankle holster.

Once it was in her hand, she looked it over. "I'm not sure what good this is gonna do."

"Then let's hope we don't need to use it. Or mine. Think you can find that page fast enough?"

She nodded. "Yeah."

"Okay. Good. Let's take my car."

***

Carson's lift turned onto the gravel drive leading to her house and pulled up behind the station wagon. She thanked the driver and stepped onto the gravel with legs that trembled. She stood in front of the house, sizing it up. Checking for anything that appeared amiss. The house was in the same sorry state it had been in yesterday when she and her parents arrived—an arrival that seemed to have happened much longer ago.

She waited for the car to drive away and slowly moved toward the front stoop. She knocked on the door. Waited. Tried the knob when no one came. It didn't give. She raised her hand to knock again, thought better about it, and went around back.

The rear door was ajar. Her guts bunched together like a fiercely tangled knot.

"Mom? Dad?" She stepped toward the door, the tightness in her belly not loosening.

Maybe the door was already like that. The place isn't in the best of shape. Maybe it can't close.

Instincts told her such reassurances were a psychic defense mechanism. With how apprehensive she'd been about moving and the new house, she would have absolutely noticed a door that wouldn't close when they arrived. It would have been one more pain point in what had already been such a painful transition.

Then why is the door open now?

At first, she remained still. Her hand found the phone Regis had given her, and she closed her fingers around it. Squeezed it.

She couldn't imagine a worse idea than entering this house. After last night, any manner of horror could be beyond that slightly open door. But she had to know if her parents were okay.

She approached the opening, cursing Regis for not touching base with her, for not letting her know it was safe to go home.

And this was her home now. For better or worse, she prayed it wasn't too late to make the most of it. To move on and rebuild.

She stepped into the house. Into darkness. Felt for a light switch. Prayed they'd gotten the power turned back on. It was a prayer God answered with a stiff *Fuck you.*

"Shit."

She left the door wide open to let as much sunlight in as possible. The shadows swallowed it in less than five paces. Her belly knotted tighter, but she took out the phone and switched on its flashlight. White LED illumination splashed across the hardwood.

"Mom! Dad! Is everyone okay?"

No response.

They might still be sleeping.

Maybe. Probably.

Hopefully.

She headed down the hallway and reached the space where the wall became a counter that separated the kitchen from the living room. She looked side to side, pointing the light to aid her vision. Both rooms looked empty, but just to be sure, she rounded the counter and checked the kitchen floor. As she looked, she did everything to not acknowledge *why* she was looking: she was checking for fallen bodies.

Slow, purposeful footsteps thumped against the hallway floor. She peered around the kitchen wall toward the front of the house. A familiar figure stood in the shadows, holding a thick clump of something in its hand. Her light beam found the figure's face.

"Ashley?" she whispered.

The girl who had come with her to the barn now had a waxy, yellow quality to her face. Her lips were pulled back—no! They'd been torn off, leaving only a ring of ragged flesh to border her teeth. Dirt was caked to enamel and the red, irritated gums. Strands of hay twisted within the gaps like stray pieces of yellow dental floss. More hay was stuffed into her tattered abdomen, writhing around the torn intestines like earthworms in a crimson, gravity-defying puddle.

Carson lowered the light to shine on the object in Ashley's hand and wished she hadn't. The light revealed her mother's severed head, still leaking gore from beneath the chin. Some of it clung to and slid down the jagged spinal cord.

The knotted tension that held Carson's belly upon first glimpsing the open back door released itself in a throat-scraping scream. The cry ripped its way out of her, riding a surging wave of bile that spilled over her tongue and sprayed through the air in a caustic arc. She backpedaled, twisted on her heel, bolted for the back door, still tasting acid as her blood pounded through her.

Ashley gave chase with a screech. She moved quickly for someone whose body had been so badly damaged. But Carson was faster.

She reached the door. Lurched over the threshold with a second cry, this one stinging less than the last.

When her feet struck the outside ground, something bit into her shoulder. Electric pain shot through her, stabbing down her left arm and into her chest like someone had injected her with liquid fire. A third scream escaped her lips. She turned toward the source of this new agony. Her ankles crossed and she stumbled, falling hard to her ass, then spilling to her back.

The clamping sharpness dislodged from her shoulder, but the pain remained hot and pulsating. Warm blood soaked through her shirt, sticking it to the surrounding flesh.

She stopped thrashing and looked up. Her mother's head levitated over her. They were face to face, with their eyes locked onto each other's. The severed neck cords leaked crimson flecks across Caron's chest, further soaking her shirt. A bubbly strand of black liquid hung from her mother's bottom lips, dangling over Carson's own mouth, threatening to seep its way inside. Noxious breath flew into Carson's face, seemingly singeing off her nose hairs and making her eyes stream.

Gold fire blossomed in the eyes above her. A tuft of something retched its way up from the back of the severed head's throat. It looked like a ball of yarn, but it expanded and contracted. A breathing tangle of living things. It was straw, a bulbous knot of it that was now rolling over the head's purple tongue.

The head was going to vomit the straw into Carson's mouth.

That's how it spreads. It's something in the straw.

The knotted foulness pressed against the back of her mother's teeth, simultaneously ballooning outward and squirming itself asunder. The golden glow changed the woman's eyes into swirling twin orbs like miniature suns. The ball of wriggling straw spread further apart, like too much spaghetti twirled onto a fork. Some of the individual strands were almost completely loose, dangling from the dead woman's lips and mingling with black drool.

Carson crossed her arms over her face, further inflaming the wound on her shoulder. She hissed and rolled to her right.

The raveled mess plopped to the dirt like a wet hairball from a prolapsed belly. It flopped and rolled with hideous life as Carson tried to press herself up using just one arm.

Ashley's form filled the doorframe. The floating head hovered in the air beside her, making figure eights like a macabre drone.

Carson groaned, she twisted, she pushed. Pain, exhaustion, and fear kept her grounded. *Vulnerable.*

She glanced from one menace to the other. Neither moved. They were toying with her. If they were capable of such cruelty in conjunction with their violence, then they were no mere animals. They were hell-spawn, just like the stories said. Demons. Literal fucking demons. And if she didn't get off her ass, she was going to become one too.

Another roll, another push, another shriek—this time at the injustice of it all.

An idea pierced its way through her panic. She was seeing her mother, she was seeing Ashley, but she wasn't seeing—

"*Daddy! Daddy, help, PLEASE!*"

Her mother's head stopped making figure eights in the air and zigzagged toward her. Teeth bared, eyes blazing. Screeching like a bird of prey.

Carson rolled left, this time forgetting the bundle of nasty her mother had spewed. She rolled on top of it, squishing the last of it flat, causing the wet hay to fan out beneath her back.

"*Daddy, please! Somebody!*"

Another figure rounded the house. Recognizing who it was, the last of her hope for survival deflated. Her father stood next to the house, but he was no longer the man who liked to *dad at his daddiest.*

A diagonal gash split his torso from his left hipbone to his right pec. An elixir of blood and that black fluid soaked his nightshirt all the way through. Lumps of organ meat spilled from the wound, bouncing off his feet like wet balls. He hooked his hands into claws and strode to Ashley's side. The severed head had returned there, now orbiting both standing vessels of the evil thing in the barn.

None of them attacked. They only watched.

Carson forced herself into a seated position. Tried again to gain her feet. Finally made it, never taking her eyes off her assailants.

Then she understood. She got it just in time to feel braided threads of straw burrowing into the wound made by her mother's teeth. The sensation was a mere discomfort compared to the pain caused by the bite. As the hay worms reached her nervous system, she felt no pain at all.

She joined her father, her mother's floating head, and her new friend from town. They stood together, like one big happy family.

Chapter 20

"Fuck," Regis said as he took a curve on 473.

Lydia looked up at him from her phone's dark screen. "What?"

"I was supposed to call somebody this morning. *Fuck.*" He smacked the heel of his hand against the steering wheel.

"Who was it?"

He told her about Carson, her wild story that turned out not to be so wild, how he'd put her up at Shady Elm and promised to call her in the morning after the deputies checked on her parents.

"They went by and talked to her father. Everything seemed to be okay. I should call her now."

He tapped on the monitor of his dashboard-mounted tablet as they took another hairpin turn. The car fishtailed and swerved into the oncoming lane. Regis cut the wheel, careful not to overcorrect. The car continued in the proper lane.

"Be careful," she said. "We don't need to wrap your car around a tree on our way to saving this shithole town."

He looked at her and gave a sideways smile. "Why did you come back if you hate it so much?"

"Because it's the right thing to do. Should've done it a long time ago."

"You were young and scared."

"You don't need to make excuses for me. I'm a mother now—I can't teach my kids to be responsible if I neglect my responsibilities."

"I guess that's why I stayed."

"You stayed to make your dad proud. You don't owe this town anything."

"Are you saying I should've run away with you?"

"I'm saying we need to be responsible. And we should also be honest with ourselves."

"It wasn't just to make him proud. I needed him to see me."

"Well, you're Sheriff now. Do you feel seen?"

"I'm following in his footsteps, but no, not really."

"Being Sheriff here is the only thing you two have in common."

"And being Black, I guess."

She chewed on her lip. "There's something about your dad you should know."

"If you're going to tell me he helped your grandmother feed that thing, don't bother. I already know, at least I do now." His jaw clenched.

"For what it's worth, I'm sorry."

"How did he do it?"

"Drug addicts. Vagrants. Any time he could pick someone up without calling it in … That thing in the barn never went hungry."

They rode the rest of the way to the West property in silence. When they got there, the officer guarding the driveway waved the car through. They stopped in front of her grandmother's house. Lydia stared at the dilapidated structure. Heat burned in her cheeks like she had a bundle of lit matches in her mouth. She clenched her fists and forced herself to breathe slowly.

Regis glanced toward her. "Are you ready?"

"Not even a little." She opened the door and got out, leaving her phone behind and saying a silent apology to Braeden—he had already called seventeen times, last she checked.

Regis followed, keeping a firm hand on the grip of his sidearm. Lydia touched the smaller firearm, which she'd tucked into her pants next to her hip. She ran her thumb along the contour of its grip. She considered taking it out as they approached the front door, but she wanted both her hands.

She pulled the door open and headed inside. A cloud that smelled of cat piss and nicotine enveloped them. She and Regis winced at the foul odor.

The shades were down, rendering their surroundings in various shades of gray. Regis brought out his flashlight and shone it around the front room. It held dusty upholstery and end tables that leaned on uneven legs. One of the ceiling fan blades was broken off, its jagged end stabbing the air like a splintery shank. A television sat on two stacks of books.

"It didn't always look like this inside," Regis said.

"No. She started neglecting the house after that night. Sometimes, she had me do dishes, but I tried not to be home."

"I remember," he said, immediately bringing her mind to late night car rides and coffee at Nana's. Back then, she tried to keep the house solely as a place to crash, sometimes not even that.

Regis shone the light into the kitchen. The leaning tower of dishes in the sink had been there a while.

"She was still living alone. How did she make so many dirty dishes?" he asked.

"I'm assuming she never did them."

Lydia tromped to her grandparents' bedroom, and Regis followed.

"Oh, Jesus," he said and covered his face with his sleeve.

"Well, that explains the smell."

A row of six litter boxes lined the wall opposite the bed. Moldy turds sat in the piss-soaked granules like fruit left to rot on the beach.

"How could anyone live like this?"

Lydia answered his question with a question. "Where are all the cats?"

"I have no idea." Regis scanned the room with his flashlight. "What we're looking for is in here?"

"Afraid so. Need to cover me from outside?"

"No, I should be all right." He sneezed so hard he dropped his flashlight.

"Are you sure? You don't need to man up on my account."

He crouched low and stood back up as soon as his knees bent to forty-five-degree angles. "Oh, fuck."

Lydia looked at him for an explanation, but he only stood there wide-eyed and holding his chest. She bent at the knees and gasped when she saw what startled him. He'd found the cats. All twelve of them. Their eyes gleamed like yellow-green jewels in the darkness.

She pulled the gun and fired it at the ceiling. The felines scattered like furry gargantuan roaches. Regis sidestepped the critters as they scampered out of the room.

Lydia set down the gun and crawled along the side of the bed toward the headboard. She dropped to her belly, wriggling her way through sand dunes of dust bunnies and under the bed. She waved some of the larger ones away and got all the way to the center of the bed. Only her legs stuck out from underneath. The claustrophobic circumstances quickened her breath.

"Lydia?" Regis asked.

"I'm okay. Just give me a few."

The cats had gathered in another room and started meowing. She reached for one of the three center floor planks and tried to get her fingers around one of its edges. Finding no purchase, she huffed and tried one of the other boards. On her next breath, some dust caught in her nose, and she sneezed.

"Bless you. A few what? A few seconds, or a few minutes?"

"A few."

Regis began to pace. The cats continued to vocalize. One or two of them yowled.

Lydia tried another board. This time, she was able to shimmy it up and take it in her hand. The coarse edge pinched her pinkie against the wall, and she cried out and dropped the board.

"What is it? What's wrong?"

"I jammed my little finger. *Ugh!*"

More cat sounds. She normally loved cats, but nothing about this made her want to pet anything with fur.

"Do you need my help?"

"Nope." She wedged her fingers around the board again, this time lifting more slowly. "Almost there."

She got both hands around it and pushed it aside. Reaching down inside the darkness, every part of her but her right arm cringed. She closed her eyes, felt around in the black.

Her fingers grasped the edge of a stack of parchments. She scrounged around until she felt certain she had all the sheets. The entire ream of it came up with a puff of older, damper dust. She pushed her way out from under the bed and got to her feet, held the manuscript against her chest as she quickly left the room. Regis followed, matching her pace.

The cats blocked their passage. She tried stepping over them, then gently nudging them with her feet, then resorted to kicking, too grossed out to feel bad about it.

Regis leapt over one of the tumbling felines. "We'd be doing them a favor if we just shot them, but I guess I'll call in animal services instead."

Lydia stepped onto the front porch, and Regis scrambled after. She sat down on the top step and lay the stack of parchment on her lap. "Oh, damn it. The gun, I left it inside."

Regis looked back inside. The cats had reconvened in the walkway. They rubbed against each other, yowling and watching the people who had just invaded their home. "It's okay; I'll get another one."

"Maybe I still need it."

Regis gave her a look.

"Or not." She began to thumb through the pages.

"You've read that whole thing?"

"Believe it or not." She flipped toward the end. "Hence why I should've done this a long time ago."

She pulled out the third page from the end. The lettering was in different sizes and so disjointed each letter could have been written by a separate hand.

"Fuck. Is that written in …?"

"Yeah, blood. Of course it's blood."

"I still have a hard time believing all this, but goddamn." He shook his head.

"Even growing up with it, it still sometimes feels … Well, let's just say that before yesterday, I could have almost convinced myself I dreamed it all up."

She ran her fingers along the lines of maroon text, searching for the right paragraph.

"You think it'd be in Latin or something."

"You met my grandparents. Do you think those old hicks could read Latin?"

"No, I guess not."

She stopped midway down the page, on a block of words about a paragraph long. She stood up, taking one page and leaving the rest.

"Found it," she said. "Let's make this fucking happen."

Chapter 21

Even in the morning light, the barn intimidated her. This looming vestige of her childhood was itself like a living thing, its door a maw she'd spent nearly all her life fearing would devour her. In a way, it had—the structure around it had overshadowed so much of her life. First, it sent her running from this place, and now it had brought her back.

Inside, the hay rippled and bulged like sinewy skin. Beneath it, the fiery yellow pulsated.

"What's it say?" Regis asked.

"It says the contract is null and void if this page were to be signed by someone from the line of whoever first made the deal. That's me. We also need a witness from the devil's side, which is why it's gotta be out here."

"It's that easy? Shit."

"I won't be signing with a pen."

"Blood?"

"You got it. Do you have a knife?"

"No."

"Not even in the car? Not even a box cutter?"

"No, who needs a knife when you have a gun, some pepper spray, and a nightstick?"

"Someone who might need one to, I don't know, cut a rope or something. You're gonna need to coldcock me."

His mouth fell open. "No fucking way."

Something under the hay made a guttural sound.

"Well, I don't want to go back in that house, do you?"

He shook his head. The thing under the hay coughed and hissed.

"I didn't think so. And I think it knows we're here, so bust my lip, and I'll use the blood."

"Okay, okay. Just ... oh, Jesus."

"I said I didn't need you to man up, but I need you to now. Either you hit me, or I'm going to do it, and I'll probably do it with that stone."

She nodded toward a jagged rock lying on the ground beside an old trough. The surface of the hay pumped like the membrane of a massive yellow heart.

"Okay, just ... Get ready."

"I'm ready."

Regis reared back and stopped. "Oh, please no."

He was looking past her, at something behind her. She turned and saw three human figures, a man and two young women. Something head-shaped circled the air around them.

"Carson," Regis said. "Oh, I'm so fucking sorry."

The figures began closing the distance, floating head leading the way. Lydia faced Regis.

"You need to do it now! Hurry!"

He drew back his fist again, tears streaming, his bottom lip trembling. This time he struck. Her vision flashed white on impact, and her legs collapsed.

As soon as she hit the ground, he rushed to her side. He cradled her head and helped her sit up. He was saying something she couldn't make out. Through blurred vision, she saw a pitchfork rise into the air beyond the barn door. Its rusty tines pointed toward them as the infected people came closer. The same yellow glow from beneath the hay glowed within their eyes.

She fumbled in the dirt for the page. Regis handed it to her, and she snatched it. With her free hand, she daubed her bloody lip with her fingertips.

"Please let this work," she said and pressed her index finger to the parchment.

The three figures halted their strides. The floating head and the pitchfork froze in midair. The straw stopped rippling, and the light below it dimmed. A chilling breeze cut through the air, carrying a sulfurous stench. Lydia and Regis exchanged glances.

"Do you think it's working?" he asked.

Lydia looked down at the paper in her hand. The blood trail in the shape of her signature brightened from red to orange. With a hissing sound, the orange spread to all the letters on the page. The parchment grew unbearably hot, and she dropped it. On its way down, flames engulfed the page. By the time it reached the ground, it was a smoldering black sheet.

"I don't know," she said.

She looked again at the figures, the levitating objects, and the barn. Regis had his gun out, both hands on it, not pointed at anything but ready to aim it at anything that got too close.

A whooshing sound made them both jolt. The source of the sound was the entire stack of parchment going up in flames back on the porch.

The floating head plopped to the ground and lay still. The pitchfork did the same, kicking up loose pieces of hay on landing. One by one, the two young women and the man buckled at the knees and collapsed, dropping on top of each other in a makeshift dogpile.

The hay stopped moving. The glow blinked out.

Regis holstered his gun, and Lydia exhaled.

"I think we did it," she said.

Regis walked toward the three crumpled figures, knelt beside them, and put his hand to Carson's neck. He sat on his butt and looked up at the sky, gritting his teeth and hugging his knees.

Lydia touched her lips. They were already swelling up and bleeding steadily. She wiped her hand on her pants and approached Regis. Put her arm around his shoulders and he leaned against her.

"I'm sorry," she said.

The barn began to tremble. Something huge smashed its way out from under the hay, bursting apart the entire front of the structure. It was a hand made of bundled straw and shards of bone.

Chapter 22

What in God's name do you think you're doing, Abram?

He shuddered awake, acid reflux stinging the back of his throat. He kicked off the comforter and sat up. He felt the throb of his heart over every section of his body. Through his limbs. Inside his head. He blinked, expecting to see his wife in the room. Could picture her perfectly, standing over him, already dressed for the day, hands on her hips and a scowl on her face as she admonished him for going on yet another bender, but—

You know damn well I'm not here about your drinking.

"You're dead, Yolanda. I watched you wither away to nothing."

That hasn't stopped you talking to me before.

He rubbed his face. "Yeah, I guess you got me there."

I know you didn't let our son go after that thing in the barn on his own. That thing in the barn you helped feed.

"He's Sheriff now. He's got the manpower. He can handle it."

If by handle it, you mean feed it a steady diet of crackheads, you don't know your son at all. He's gonna want to stop it. Won't be surprised if he called Lydia to help.

"Lydia? Al West's granddaughter? She moved away."

No one stays away from a past like hers forever. And you know what I mean. All your drinking and passing out while watching old wrestling shows don't numb the pain the way it used to, does it? Your coping mecha-

nisms are failing you because you know you don't wanna die with unfinished business on your conscience.

"I thought this wasn't about my drinking."

It isn't.

He looked directly at the spot where he imagined she would be standing if ovarian cancer hadn't eaten her alive. "I miss you."

I miss you too. But what I don't miss is watching you feel sorry for yourself. I don't miss knowing what you were doing in your last few years as Sheriff.

"You knew about it?"

I know now.

"Of course you do. You're only real inside my head."

Maybe I am, maybe I'm not. If I am just a hallucination, I wouldn't be saying what I'm saying, unless you knew I was right.

He didn't have a response for that. He grabbed for the beer he'd left on his nightstand, remembered Regis taking it from him. "Son of a bitch."

Don't be so hard on yourself. Unless you aren't planning on doing the right thing today.

"The right thing."

Don't pretend like you don't know what that is. And who knows? Maybe at the end of it all, you'll get to see me again.

He looked down at his lap, stained underwear, filthy socks. Looked back at where she might be standing. "I'd like that, baby."

I would too. Now get your crusty ass up off that bed and go help our son.

He nodded and put his feet on the floor. "Yeah. Yeah, I guess I'm gonna go do that."

He shuffled toward the bedroom door.

Hey, Abram?

He stopped, looked back even though she wasn't there.

I love you.

"I love you too, baby. I love you too."

Chapter 23

Another huge hand of straw and bone pushed its way up from the ground and shoved its way through a side wall. Several planks splintered as they scattered through the air with tufts of straw. The hand slapped the nearby earth, causing the ground under their feet to tremble. Regis redrew his gun and pointed it at the barn. Clumps of earth and straw parted for the creature's bulbous head.

"Dear God," Lydia said.

The creature opened its eyes slowly, like a newborn. Yellow-orange fire churned within like infernal spiral galaxies. Its lips spread to reveal white teeth shaped like corkscrews.

Regis pointed the gun at its left eye. Fired. Caught the creature in the lower left forehead.

Someone grabbed him by the wrist. Lydia. She pulled him toward the car as the creature's shoulder and chest emerged, breaking apart the barn's roof and remaining walls like they were made of popsicle sticks. They ran across the rumbling ground, staggering to keep their feet.

The creature pressed itself out of the hole. The ground around the wreckage of the structure cracked, massive fissures that split the earth like sunbaked ground after months without rain. But the cracks kept spreading, reaching toward Lydia and Regis as they bolted toward the vehicle. One of the creature's knees struck the hole, causing a vibration that took Regis off his feet. He stumbled into Lydia. Their limbs tangled, and he fell atop her.

He struggled to get up as another vibration shook the earth. Lydia pushed on his chest while he pushed against the ground. He fell again, this time knocking their heads together. The impact hurt more than it should've, given the short distance, but it also woke him up, brought a clarity he hadn't felt since the monster began to emerge.

He rolled and sat up. Lydia sat up beside him. They clasped hands and resumed running.

The creature was all the way out now, scanning its surroundings for its first victim. The bodies of Carson, the other girl, and the guy all began sliding toward its nearest foot. The severed head tumbled after them like a battered, half-deflated ball, strings of blood-soaked hair waving in the wind along its bounding journey.

Lydia and Regis ran past her grandmother's house. It, too, was collapsing. Falling in on itself like a wet carboard box under an unseen foot. The cats inside screeched and yowled. Two made it onto the porch but were consumed when its planks caved in, burying the pets under rotted wood and rusty nails.

The fallen corpses and the severed head reached the creature's foot. Tendrils of hay snatched them, wrapping around them like creeping vines in sped-up motion. They were pulled inside, becoming part of the creature. A silent explosion of orange expanded across the entry point.

Lydia and Regis reached the car just as the creature spotted them. It lurched toward them on long, angled legs. The earth cracked and sunk in under every titanic step. The creature bared its teeth again and let out a gurgling hiss so loud that they both needed to cover their ears. They each opened the door and slid into their seats. The creature was close now, a hulking figure in the rearview, much closer than it appeared, something like magma burning at the back of its throat.

With a swipe of its clawed hand, the light bar atop the cruiser shattered. The incessant, sharp plinking of falling glass and claws scraping the metal roof made Regis grind his back teeth. He fumbled for the keys, while Lydia smacked a tattoo on the dashboard, desperate for him to start the car.

He stuck the key in the ignition. The creature struck the car again.

This time, the vehicle went end over end, jostling them in their seats. Unrestrained, they smacked into each other. Smacked the seatbacks. Smacked the wheel and the dashboard.

The car came to rest on its side. Lydia had fallen out of her seat, pinning Regis against the door and driver's side window.

Through swimming vision, Regis saw the creature head up the hill between Lydia's house and the one recently occupied by Carson's family. It was headed toward town. His gaze drifted to the dashboard clock. Barnyard Days had just begun.

"Lydia," he slurred. "Lydia, wake up. We gotta go after it."

She moaned and stirred. Blood leaked from the corner of her mouth, mixing with the drying crimson of her busted lip. He tried to push her off him, but she was dead weight and wouldn't wake.

"Come on, Lydia. Main Street's full of people. They're all going to fucking die."

She shook her head slowly. Winced against consciousness. Her eyes opened. "Regis? What are we … how …"

"We're in trouble. Reaper's Bend is in trouble. We gotta get out of this car."

Though the creature had likely reached 473 by now, its footsteps still sounded thunderous, like a passing storm.

Lydia blinked and looked around. Frowned and looked at Regis for an explanation.

"The thing from the barn," he said. "It's out."

Her frown loosened as memories returned. She nodded, slowly at first but then more rapidly. She looked up at the passenger door and began to climb.

Chapter 24

People heard it before they felt it. Felt it before they saw it. The first people who saw it had mixed reactions. Some stared at the approaching creature in a mix of awe, terror, and disbelief. Others turned and ran screaming into the tightly packed crowd, including one of the two deputies posted up at the closest end of Main Street.

The deputy who stood his ground pulled his gun and pointed it at the creature. Given its size, he frantically scanned its body for a weak point.

The creature scooped up a nearby sedan and hurled it, bowling over gathered people like pins at the end of a lane. It struck the gun-wielding deputy first, bursting apart his torso like a gore-filled water balloon before crashing and flipping. The rolling vehicle crushed people beneath it, flattening them to bloody human-shaped pancakes on the pavement in front of Nana's Diner. The projectile merely clipped other bystanders, but they were no luckier. It knocked them aside, flinging them into windows of neighboring businesses and tumbling them across pavement and concrete.

The car came to rest in front of the butcher shop, appropriately dressed in ruined meat and streaked red. The bedlam turned heads. Now everyone saw the creature, and panic erupted on Main Street.

***

After pushing the car back onto its wheels, Lydia and Regis drove into town and arrived in time to see the creature take a bite out of someone it held in its hand. The bite ripped off everything from the diaphragm up on the creature's victim. Blood squirted from the remnants in the creature's hand, and entrails drooled from the creature's pointed chin as it chewed with its corkscrew teeth.

"This is all my fault," Lydia said. "I should've ... I ... oh, God."

"None of that now." Regis held up his sidearm. "Can you shoot?"

Lydia felt the back of her head, feeling an egg-shaped bump next to her right ear. She winced but nodded.

"Then here. Don't lose this one."

She turned it over in her hand. "What is this gonna do against that?"

"I don't know, but we've got to try." He put his hand on the rifle. "I'm gonna get up close and take out its kneecaps. When it's down, I want you to shoot out the fucker's eyes. If it takes all goddamn day, you and I are gonna take this monster apart."

She nodded, and it made her head throb even worse. They got out of the banged-up car and walked toward the marauding monstrosity. So many dead lay in its wake, stretched before them like cattle in an outdoor slaughterhouse. Entrails and blood paved the road. Some broken bodies were still alive, twitching and moaning in exquisite agony. Coughing up blood. Crawling away from the nightmare on the street and dragging broken legs behind them. Stumbling around with leaking headwounds. Faces and exposed flesh dusted with gravel and skinned by road rash.

Windows of nearby businesses were either shattered or splashed with gore. More able-bodied survivors ran away from the carnage. The creature threw the lower section of the body in its hand, dropping several of the runners and spattering them with crimson.

For a horrible moment, Lydia got the notion that she'd died and gone to hell. She would never see Braeden again. Never tuck Roger and Annabelle in again.

Regis put a stabilizing hand on her shoulder. He cradled the shotgun with the other. "I'm gonna go on ahead. You hang back here until I shoot out its legs."

"No way." She shook her head.

"I'm telling you, it's the only plan I got. Do you have any other ideas?"

She thought of the burning pages. The bodies of the possessed sliding toward the monster's foot before being immersed into its infernal bloodstream.

"We already tried my plan. Look where it got us."

"You can't blame yourself. Let's just ... do what we can to make it right."

She cast another grim look at the bodies littering the street. She didn't know if there was any coming back from this, but she nodded nonetheless. "Be careful, okay?"

"I will." He released her and jogged after the creature.

Lydia ducked behind a battered van. The vehicle was less splattered with human remains than the others but still not entirely clean. A human hand, torn through at the forearm, lay on the hood, its ragged stump still leaking. Chunks floated in a red puddle less than two feet from where she was posted. She looked past the severed limb to watch Regis approach the creature. His hand was close enough to the trigger guard for him to take aim and fire in a pinch.

The creature swiped the ground, impaling an elderly woman through the chest on its forefinger. It flung her aside, and she crashed into a parking meter, bending in half around its post. Her limbs spasmed as she spat out wads of blood.

Regis was nearly close enough now for a fired round from his shotgun to matter, but not just yet. The creature still hadn't turned on him.

Maybe this plan would work after all.

Lydia forced herself to watch. Blocked out the pain. Ignored the hope that this might soon be over. No distractions. She needed to be ready to attack when it was time. She prayed this plan would work better than signing her name in blood.

She should've known it'd be too easy.

The creature kicked aside another slower victim. Sent the body cartwheeling through the air and smashing against a brick wall. The man's body fell like a pile of clothes onto the sidewalk, as if every bone had shattered on impact.

Lydia clenched the gun until her knuckles turned white.

Regis stopped and raised the shotgun. Pointed it at the back of the creature's left knee. Squeezed the trigger. A fist-sized section of leg burst apart, gushing black fluid. The creature dropped to one knee with thunderous impact that shook the street.

"Yes!" she cried out.

Despite all the death around them, excitement surged through her, and she emerged from her hiding place. The creature stood, and her enthusiasm drained.

Regis fired again at the same area. This time, the bullet caught the back of the creature's thigh, causing the eruption of more black blood.

The creature turned toward them, eyes and brow bent downward in anger. It was hurt, though, was limping.

Regis targeted the same leg, this time aiming at the kneecap. He fired, now at an even closer range, and the knee exploded.

The creature went down. On its way, it swung an open hand.

The claw-tipped fingers clipped Regis, knocking the shotgun from his hands and sending him rolling across the street. His hip struck the curb, and he yelled his pain through gritted teeth.

The creature was propped up on its arms and belly. Its eyes blazed with fury. Twisted teeth gnashed at the air as it bellowed and screeched.

Lydia marched toward it, screaming as she unloaded the Glock into its face. Rapid-fire curse words and rage-fueled cries sailed toward the beast with every round. Quarter-sized black holes opened across its cheeks, forehead, and chin. The creature shook its head side to side and shrieked.

Lydia dislodged the spent magazine and rushed to Regis's side. He already had the reload ready, holding it out for her as his pained breath seethed.

"Try getting its eyes," he said.

"What the hell do you think I'm trying to do?" She slammed in the magazine and pointed the weapon at the creature's face. "Die, you fucker."

She fired again and again. This time, she hit its left eye. The orange substance flowed from the new opening like lava from a volcanic vent.

The creature pressed itself up, its left leg reattached. A cry tinged with pain and triumph tore through the air over Main Street. It lifted its leg to crush Lydia under its foot.

She tucked and rolled, losing the gun in the process and landing with a thump against the tire of a gore-covered pickup truck. She tried to stand but fell to her butt, dropped by dizziness, pain, and vibrations from the step that nearly crushed her. She opened her eyes to see Regis crawling toward her, hand outstretched. The creature towered over them, the living embodiment of imminent death.

Lydia reached for Regis. The creature reached for them.

"Hey," came a holler from somewhere on the street.

The creature turned toward the call. Lydia and Regis followed its gaze.

"Dad," Regis said.

The creature returned its attention to Lydia and Regis. Gave them another view of its teeth. The bone-white protrusions were draped in rags of flesh and masticated entrails.

"I know you heard me, motherfucker," Abram Jones said.

He had no weapons. One arthritic finger was pointed up at the creature. His other hand was unbuttoning his shirt.

***

Regis forced himself to sit up as his father kept coming from the opposite end of Main Street. He tried to stand, but he was too spent, too hurt. "What's he doing?"

"I'm not sure," Lydia said.

She was sitting now too. They held each other and watched, too weakened to do anything beyond that. Just ten seconds ago, they'd been resigned to certain death.

"Don't you recognize me?" Abram undid another button. "I only fed your diabolical ass every day for ten damn years."

The creature took a step toward him. He undid another button.

"That's right, devil. Come to Daddy."

The creature cocked its head to the right and flexed its fingers. Raised one foot to take another step. Paused.

"You're so used to people running from you, you don't know what to do when someone comes at you."

Abram took his shirt in both hands and ripped it open.

"My God," Regis said.

His father's torso was covered in symbols, symbols like the one etched onto the barn door. These weren't drawings, though. They were scars. His father had done this to himself. A long time ago, from the looks of it. Twisted black ridges made shapes with too many points. Even his back was marked, somehow.

"All right, you ugly spawn of Satan. It's chow time."

"Dad, don't!" Regis yelled.

The creature started to look over its shoulder.

"Don't look at them, fool. Look at me. I'm talking to you. And I know you're hungry. You may think you're insatiable, but you won't be starving after you eat my old ass. Come on, motherfucker."

The creature refocused on him. Hooked its fingers.

"Those symbols," Lydia said. "They may actually hurt it."

"Don't even say that," Regis said, trying again to stand. The pain flared in his hip and dragged him back down. "Don't even ... Dad, please!"

"I love you, Regis," Abram said.

The creature loomed over him, parting its jaws.

"Then don't do this."

"I'm not doing nothing but my job."

But I'm Sheriff now, Regis thought but lost the will to say. *It's on me.*

Lydia squeezed him tightly. He rested his head on her shoulder but couldn't look away from what was about to go down.

"Come and get it, asshole," Abram said.

The creature reared back its head and chomped down onto Abram's upper half. Its teeth pierced his belly and back, rending flesh and crunching bone. When it lifted him into the air, blood fell like rain from a single cloud. It opened its mouth again, closing its lips around Abram's legs. It swallowed him with a sickening gulp.

At first, nothing happened. The creature retrained its sights on Lydia and Regis. The dead bodies and broken pieces of people slid along the street toward it, soon to be absorbed.

Lydia and Regis struggled to their feet, fighting through the pain and preparing to run, even though it was unlikely they could outpace this creature for even a few seconds. They were too hurt, and its legs were too long.

But the creature stopped coming. It stood in the middle of Main Street with clawed hands at its sides and its face snarling. Orange expanded at the center of its body like a growing cloud at sunset. The fire spread beneath its hay-covered skin, setting its entire torso aglow.

"We need to take cover," Regis said.

Lydia nodded, and they limped together, falling between two of the nearest buildings. They each covered their ears in time for the concussive blast of the creature blowing apart. Sloppy chunks of black and orange flew all over Main, some of it splattering the alley where Lydia and Regis had fallen. Within the ruined parts, strands of hay writhed and sizzled as they burned, and the orange iridescence went dark.

Epilogue

Lydia dialed Braeden's number from the hospital bed. When he didn't answer, she sighed and dropped her head back on the pillow. She figured he would be mad, but not *this* mad.

She found the remote and thumbed through some of the channels the hospital offered. Cop show. Horror movie. Romance. Reality TV. None of it held her interest. She switched the television off and tried to fall asleep. Surprisingly, it worked.

***

When she woke, a man in a solid red outfit was sitting in the chair beside her bed. He grinned when she opened her eyes. She didn't recognize him until he spoke.

"It looks like you could use my help," the man said.

"Like you helped my family, right? No thanks."

"Come now. You haven't even heard my spiel yet. How about this: I won't force you to keep one of my fallen in your barn and feed it whenever it gets hungry."

"Easy enough. I don't have a barn."

"You know what I mean. And I'm not such a bad guy. I just want to make sure you see your family again."

"How about this: go fuck yourself."

The devil laughed at her rebuke. Sleep took her again.

***

"Mommy?"

Roger's voice pulled her out of the depths. He was standing beside her. Braeden stood behind him, holding Annabelle.

"Are you guys really here?" she asked.

"They sure are," someone said from the doorway.

It was Regis, leaning on a pair of crutches.

"Oh, thank God." She met her husband's gaze. "I'm so sorry. I ..."

"Don't be," Braeden said. "You can explain yourself later. Now, I'm just glad you're alive."

"Okay. Thank you."

"Your sheriff friend showed us which room you were in," Roger said.

"That's right," Regis said with a small nod. There was slight disappointment in his eyes that only she could detect. "Well, I'll let you get to catching up." He turned to leave.

"Hey, wait a minute," Lydia said. "What about Reaper's Bend?"

He gave her a wry smile. "We're gonna put it back together a piece at a time. I've already started working on it with some good people. There wouldn't be any town at all if you hadn't come.

"Is Mommy a superhero?" Roger asked.

She ruffled his hair. "Sheriff Regis is just being nice."

Regis nodded at her. "Take care of yourself, Lydia." He nodded at Braeden. "Sir."

"Is Mama okay?" Annabelle asked.

Her family looked at her as Regis left the doorway. Lydia searched her thoughts for the answer. She looked from one member of her family to the other, her gaze coming to rest on Braeden, whose face showed the most concern.

Finally, she said, "Mama's fine, sweetheart. Mama's just fine."

***

Regis settled back in his hospital bed and covered himself with the sheet. The medicine had done a nice job numbing the pain, and he thought he might even manage to get some sleep. He looked at the chair and dresser inside his room. Several gifts were piled there. Flowers from the library staff, some cards, a bottle of merlot from the surviving deputies. There were even several wrapped gifts, but his gaze stopped on a rectangular leather box no larger than a thick book.

This was not a gift. It was more like something left in his charge.

It had been given to him in exchange for some extra help rebuilding the town. The man in red had promised Regis wouldn't have to feed it. That was the only reason he'd agreed. While all too true that the devil always lied, Regis felt confident that he could handle whatever his new charge would require. And if it didn't get out of control, he was sure his father would be proud.

About the author

Lucas Mangum is the author of several books, including *Gods of the Dark Web, Saint Sadist*, and the forthcoming *Haunted Hearts*. He lives in Austin with his family. When he's not writing about deals with the devil and human scarecrows, he's reading, camping, or finding new places to hide the bodies. For more information, go to LMHorror.com.

Milton Keynes UK
Ingram Content Group UK Ltd.
UKHW020251220424
441462UK00005B/80/J